All of Me

CHRIS BARON

Feiwel and Friends

New York

A Feiwel and Friends Book
An imprint of Macmillan Publishing Group, LLC
175 Fifth Avenue, New York, NY 10010

Our books may be purchased in bulk for promotional, educational, or business
use. Please contact your local bookseller or the Macmillan Corporate and
Premium Sales Department at (800) 221-7945 ext. 5442 or by email at
MacmillanSpecialMarkets@macmillan.com.

Library of Congress Cataloging-in-Publication Data

Names: Baron, Chris, author.
Title: All of me / Chris Baron.
Description: First edition. | New York : Feiwel and Friends, 2019. |
    Summary: Ari faces what it is to be a man while dealing with a cross-country
    move, his parents' separation, being bullied for his weight, and belatedly
    starting bar mitzvah preparations.
Identifiers: LCCN 2018039332| ISBN 978-1-250-30598-5 (hardcover) |
    ISBN 978-1-250-30599-2 (ebook)
Subjects: | CYAC: Novels in verse. | Body image—Fiction. | Overweight
    persons—Fiction. | Jews—United States—Fiction. | Bar mitzvah—Fiction. |
    Bullying—Fiction. | Family problems—Fiction. | Moving, Household—Fiction.
Classification: LCC PZ7.5.B37 All 2019 | DDC [Fic]—dc23
LC record available at https://lccn.loc.gov/2018039332

Book design by Eileen Savage

Feiwel and Friends logo designed by Filomena Tuosto

First edition, 2019

10 9 8 7 6 5 4 3 2 1

mackids.com

For my dear family, Ella, Asa,
Samaria, and Caylao,
and for anyone doing their
best to be all of who
they are.

Before Summer

Who Am I?

The life in my head seems
so different from the life outside,
where I am so big
that everyone stares,
but no one sees the real me.

My name is Ari Rosensweig.
This year, I am the newest seventh grader
at Mill Valley Middle School.
I have sandy-brown hair
and green eyes like my father's.
I'm average height, but

I am a fat kid, and I hate it when
people call me names.

Even though I'm overweight,
I can still do everything
everyone else can—
ride my bike, play video games—
but people just see me as different,
only notice who I am
on the outside.

My mother is an artist
who sculpts giants in clay
and paints the world
on canvas, on murals,
and even on clothes;
my father sells what she paints.
I'm an only child.
Sometimes I get lonely,
wish for a brother or sister,
but I get so much time to myself
to do what I like to do,
and no one interferes.

I make role-playing games.
I'm going to be a cryptozoologist.
I want to find the creatures out there,
like Bigfoot, that might seem so different
but that belong to this world too.

My mother says we are going
to spend the summer at the beach;
Out in nature, she says.
I like the beach, but I don't like
taking off my shirt.

I always have to hike up my pants,
and I worry that there isn't enough food,
because I'm always hungry.
More than anything, I think,
I want to lose weight,
and I don't know how.

Why Are You So Fat?
people always ask (not always out loud)

I'm not fat.
I sit up straighter,
feel the rolls on my body unbuckle.
I just have big bones. That's what my mom says.
I have big bones and bigger spaces in between them.
        Why are you so fat?
Well, they say my grandfather, from eastern Europe
had a mysterious disease that made him big;
he carried it with him,
and he gave it to my mother
and my mom had it and now I have it.
        Why are you so fat?
Because my grandmother made me eat every bite,
told me to never leave anything on my plate.
        Why are you so fat?
It's a gland problem.
I've got bad glands.
Someone told me about glands,
so I think I have bad ones.
        Why are you so fat?

The doctor says I can't help it.
He says I may not look normal,
but I'm healthy enough to carry the stars,
and this fat keeps me safe.
    Why are you so fat?
Because I love school lunches: meat pies and yogurt cups
and a giant cookie, and then after school
I take the five dollars my parents give me
and buy slices of pizza from Mario's and play the old Pac-
    Man machine until dark,
stack quarters along the edge
until I pass the second apple.
    Why are you so fat?
My parents are never really home anyway.
They're busy,
and I fill myself up with food and watching TV,
comic books, and going to the park, and hot dogs with
    ketchup and onions.
    Why are you so fat?
Sometimes I get home to an empty apartment
and the echo of the cars going by on the street outside.
    Why are you so fat?
Because if someone asks enough times,
then the question becomes the answer.

Moving

When your mother is an artist,
you move a lot.
We stretched ourselves
across the whole country
from New York to San Francisco,

far from our family
and everything we knew.

For the artist,
making a new life
is as simple
as scraping off a palette,
setting up a new studio.

For me
the studio means
quiet corners
with slabs of clay,
sketch pads
and universes,
hands and face chalked
with pastels, potato chip grease,
and Pepsi.
     Spider-Man comics,
The Hobbit, and *Bridge to Terabithia*.
For me it means waiting.
It means space,
suspended in time
between the mother
who is the Artist,
the father who is too busy,
and a son
whose story is about being
the new kid in seventh grade,
awkward, big, different
from everyone else.

Since Leaving New York

we haven't celebrated
the high holidays like we used to,
with the rest of the family.
It's like things that used to matter
suddenly don't anymore.

I didn't know I cared.
I thought of it as something we just did,
who we are, but now that it's gone,
I think about those long tables
back in New York,
overflowing with food
and candles at Shabbat,
and the grown-ups
talking long into the night,
the cousins playing ring-a-levio
outside, or capture the flag.

When we left,
they stopped talking to us,
or we stopped talking to them,
like we were all suddenly
not in the same story anymore.

When I tell this to my father
on the way to the rabbi's office,
his eyes get wet,
          so I don't say anything else.

Rabbi's Office

Right away I am nervous
because we are already
a year late in the process
of my bar mitzvah because my parents
just didn't make the time.
My father waits outside,
and I go in.

The first thing I notice
is a little glass globe.
Inside is a blue river
and green trees in the center,
a whole world, so peaceful,
a storybook inside glass.

If I could, I would sleep
next to the trunk of the tree
closest to the rock,
where words are etched
in delicate precision:

> "I will pour water on the thirsty land,
> and streams on the dry ground."

The rabbi tells me that his grandson
brought the globe back from Israel.
He lets me hold it.

He gives me saltwater taffy.
He's calm,
and everything he says

sounds like a story
I might be a part of.
I make promises to practice,
and he writes down some dates
for when to come back,
all the way through the summer.
It's a good meeting. A start at least.
It won't be the worst thing
to come here.

Grown-Up Talk

In my room, I watch
The Greatest American Hero.
It's an old show
I watch with my dad about these aliens who
give a suit to some guy
and it makes him a superhero.
I think about what I would do
if I had the suit.
How I would fight for good.
How I would streak across the sky.
How I might look in that skintight suit.
I would have to get in shape and exercise,
or maybe the suit would change me
just by my putting it on.

I hear my parents
talking in a low hum
in the dining room,
a gentle
stream of words

flowing through the house.
It's comfort,
the uncomplicated vibration
of grown-up talk,
the sound, not the words.

But then, in the middle of the second commercial,
I hear a crashing sound,
the dining room table, the pewter cup,
the dinner dishes falling.
The bass of my father's yell vibrates
through the wall.
I hear the shriek
of my mother's angriest voice.
I hear
    crashing,
        bumps,
                door slams.
I hide in my room and wait.
The Greatest American Hero
slides under a car
to stop it from crashing
into a school bus.
My parents yell,
but it's when I hear crying
that I try to be brave.
I open my door,
sneak down the very short hallway
until the sound burns like fire.
My father sits on top of my mother,
holds her head down,
screaming, *Fatso, you're killing me!*
She screams back

every word
I have been told
not to say.
Other words too,
about traveling,
about lying again,
another woman's name,
about businesses. About money.
Words in spit and terrible angles.
His body hangs over her,
his weight over hers, trying to maneuver
their awkward, swollen adult bodies.

I want to rush in and knock him over.
I want her to stop screaming.

I've heard yelling before,
always shouting at each other
as if this pitch and fury
is just a part of who they are,
but I've never seen them like this before.

When my father finally notices me, his eyes are broken,
pleading, guilty, hopeless.
She's driving me crazy, he says.
He stops, stand ups, grabs his cigarettes,
walks out of the apartment.

My mother gets off the floor too,
stops crying,
tries to pull herself together,
takes a drink of whatever is on the table,

stares at the door, left slightly open.
Grown-up talk, Ari, she says,
and sits down in her chair.
Just grown-up talk.

School over the Bridge

I should be going
to school in San Francisco,
where we live,
but my parents
send me over the Golden Gate,
to Mill Valley Middle School.

They say they want to send me to the *best* school.
It's won all the awards, my mother tells me.

I ask her if she'll get me a phone now
since I will be going so far every day,
but she tells me, *No!*
Under no circumstances, she says.
Those things stifle creativity!
You can always reach me on the school phone.

At first, my father drove me every day,
and we laughed and talked about school
or the family in New York
or the best ways to talk to girls,
but after doing it for a while,
I could tell he didn't like
driving over the bridge every day.

One day he got really quiet,
played the music a little louder,
and we didn't talk at all.
This drive is too long, he said.
There's got to be another way.

I Will Fight You
Words are the source of misunderstandings.
—Antoine de Saint-Exupéry, The Little Prince

When you are fat,
you get picked on.
It's just how it is,
especially if you're the new kid.
I don't know what to say
most of the time.

I just want them to like me.
I want to fit in.

At the Ping-Pong table
before school,
Frank tells me
that he is afraid of Mark,
that he made him mad somehow.

Frank's one of the people
I see before school,
because his parents drop him early
for the breakfast program,
and sometimes I get there early too.

We eat doughnuts between games,
and I eat way too many.
Powdered sugar
wafts onto the table,
white flecks
on a green field.

I want Frank to be my friend
but usually he is mean to me,
picks me last at PE,
makes fat jokes,
even pushes me.
Sometimes, on bad
days, he chases
me on the bike path after school.

One time he called me "Jewboy."
When I told my parents,
they said to stay away,
but there is
nowhere else
to go.

For now, we are
battling on the table,
and for once I am winning.
You're pretty good, he says.
I used to have a table at home, I reply.
I didn't. I try not to lie,
but I'm scared to tell him
that I learned to play
with my parents, in New York,

on vacation in the Catskills
and at Camp Shalom.
I don't want him
to ask me questions
about being Jewish.

Mark is weak, I say between serves.

Mark is not weak. Not at all.
The mini-doughnut wrapper blows across
the table. Powdered sugar
covers the green field, the paddles, our hands.

You are way tougher, I insist.
Frank *is* strong, but not the toughest,
maybe in the bottom of the top ten,
behind the obvious choices,
mixed in with the dark-horse contenders,
strong kids, good athletes,
kids who do karate and kung fu.

I tell Frank that he can kick
Mark's ass, that he shouldn't worry.

The bell rings.
Frank smiles and grabs his bag.
Later, he says.
I feel the pride of helping,
and soon, in my mind,
I am standing on the far field,
across from the basketball courts,
right alongside him and the other cool kids.

....

I see Frank later in PE.
He stands next to Mark.
They are looking at me and laughing.
Mark is the tallest in the class.
In the mile run,
he glides past us
like some action hero.
Crushes baseballs,
spirals footballs.

After lunch, in the bathroom,
Brian Yee whispers to me,
I hear Mark and Frank are going to kick your butt.

Why did I open my big mouth?
I meant well.
I just didn't think past that moment,
that I was the outsider,
but I can't go through people
to get inside.
I don't fit into those spaces,
no matter how much I lie to myself.
I am too big,
even in theory,
to hide,
    too slow
        to run.
I shouldn't have said anything.

   We're gonna get you, Fatboy, they say.

How long do I have?

First Friend

On one of my first days
in this new school,
the counselor ducks me into class,
unannounced, sits me near the back,
close to a wiry, brown-haired kid
with bright eyes and a square jaw.

I'm John, he says.
Ari, I reply.

His desk is filled with notebook pages
of robots and mechs from *Transformers*,
Robotech, *Voltron*, and *Battle of the Planets*
drawn in blue pen and scratched eraser marks.

I watch him smear ChapStick on his lips every ten
        minutes,
even digging out the last bits of lip balm with a
        toothpick.
One day, John drops the toothpick
on the floor and mumbles, *My pick . . .*
And that's where it really starts.
For a while, I try to call him ChapStick,
or Chap, Bot, or anything else he might like better,
but it always becomes the nickname
            Pick.

Finding the nickname
finally made me feel like I lived here,
like we shared something just between us.

. . . .

Pretty soon it's me and Pick all the time,
watching cartoons together on long Saturday mornings,
Spider-Man, *The Transformers*, *Avatar*,
and Pick's favorite,
an old anime called *G-Force*.
I love 7-Zark-7, he says,
a round, trash-can-looking robot
who is always afraid
but who helps protect Earth
from nine hundred fathoms below the sea.

Dolan Avenue House

Halfway through the year,
my father starts to spend
his days and nights
in the garment district,
selling the hand-painted
clothes my mother designs.
He tells me once,
on his way to work,
This is how we survive.
I hardly see him.

They let me
take the bus now,
over the Golden Gate
on Sunday nights
to stay with Pick's
family on Dolan Avenue
off Shoreline Highway
a few days a week.

They even bought
me a bike to keep
at Pick's house.

Every day, from the house,
we ride our bikes
to school along
the bike path,
through the marsh.

At first,
it feels like
long sleepovers,
whispering stories
in the dark,
learning not
to be alone.
This family, so kind to me,
even though they pack
mostly gross vegetables for lunch,
eat salads every day,
eat nearly invisible
portions at dinner,
even though I am
always starving.

The First Time I Meet Lisa

I spin the combo
on my bike lock,
but it won't open.
I breathe heavy

and groan in frustration.
The first bell is about to ring.

Frank laughs as he walks by.
What's the matter—
are your fingers too fat
for the lock?

I don't look.

Why don't you just shut up.
I hear her voice
like a bolt of lightning.

The lock pops open.

Her long blond hair
shines against her green
military jacket,
her arms filled with books.

She puts out her hand
with a thousand silver bracelets.
I'm Lisa.
But I know this.
I saw her my very first day,
the rebel girl
who misses school sometimes,
who looks like she's in high school.

I'm Ari, and we shake,
walk toward the bike racks.

. . . .

How is it being the new kid?
Oh, it's great, I lie.
She looks at me
like she's waiting for the joke to end.
Where did you move from?
New York, I say.
Wow, she says. *I wanna go there one day.*
You know, I say, *it's a grid.*
What? She looks at me.
A grid.
You know, the way the city is built,
like on a big sheet of graph paper.

Like this? Lisa opens a journal
filled with blue-and-white graph paper
with drawings of dragons, and daggers,
and castles against dark skies.

Wow, those are amazing.
Thanks. She smiles,
turns to walk toward class.
I blurt out,
Hey, we are making a game
about giant robots!
Cool, she says.
Maybe you can show me some time?

She waves with her notebook,
so comfortable
in her own body,
curves and all.
I can tell because

I'm an expert
in uncomfortable.

> *Bye, Ari!*
> and she runs
> toward her homeroom.

Pencil Space

I am box-shaped.
I waddle when I walk.
When I sit down,
my sides
squirt out from my pants
and create a ridge.
The skin on the surface of that ridge
must aggravate the nerve endings,
because it can feel the metal
part of the school chair.
In class, I take my pencil,
lay it between the edge of the desk
and my stomach and measure
in a T-shape
the distance in between,
how many pencils of space
between my stomach and the desk.
For Mark, two at least,
For Diana, at least two and a half.
For me, less than one,
even when I suck it in,
even when I push my jacket into my body,

less than one pencil space.
Carlos, no pencil space at all,
gets stuck when he tries to stand up too fast.
Other kids say he's been like that since first grade.
They leave him alone now,
like they don't even see him anymore,
like he doesn't exist,
but that seems worse.

In the mornings,
kids sit sideways in their desks.
Pick is talking to Abra,
and Noah is laughing at something
that Grace just told him,
moving his body freely up and down,
his legs crossed, comfortable;
I see the angles of his body
with space all around.
When Skye talks to me,
I wish so badly I could
sit sideways in my chair.
I want to turn around
and see her eyes.
She always smells like candy.
I turn as much as I can,
my stomach pressed against
the wood lip of the desk,
my neck aching.
I want this one simple thing
to open up more space
between my desk and my body,
to stop seeing
life in pencil lengths.

Shadow Father

By the end of seventh grade,
my father becomes a shadow,
tired, distant,
weighted down,
the business swollen,
sculptures,
paintings,
and prints,
and hand-painted dresses,
my mom's designs
arcing across
silk and cotton,
a life fleeced
with fabric,
the world puffed up
in San Francisco showrooms
and design expos,
important meetings
way past my bedtime.

One weekend day before summer,
I go with my mom to the giant warehouse
where they make everything.
I have something to tell everyone,
she says, *and I want you with me, Ari.*

I love the warehouse,
acrylic paints and oil slicks,
messy palettes, blue jeans,
bundled fabric, stacked canvases

like bright packages
waiting to be ripped open,
and jars of brushes
in water pots planted on
gesso-stained coffee tables
and wooden supermarket crates.
The sinks in the back,
swirled into muddy rainbows.

She floats inside
like she has wings for real.
Her paintbrush poised as always
for correction and for instruction,
forever the mentor
where artists work
to repeat her designs now on shower curtains,
pillowcases, sweatshirts, and blankets,
each one original, each one
poured out from the well
of a single imagination.

I run ahead of her
into my father's office,
a goliath door
in the center of the work space,
I unhitch the latch, push.

This is the first time I see her,
his assistant, on the leather couch,
her legs crossed,
my father pacing.
Ari? he says, surprised, and pulls me in,

sits me in his desk chair,
gives me the name of the woman on the couch,
who smiles as if she knows me.

Look at all these orders!
Bright-white paper scratched with squid ink,
some numbers and names unrecognizable,
stacked and folded in uncertain order.

The Artist ignores him,
moves from table to table
in an unbreakable orbit.
This will be her last day
of showing everyone
how to paint her designs,
of overseeing other artists,
of meetings and questions
and business that she doesn't understand.
Spirits beg for her to release them
into terra-cotta and canvas.

I'm going to work on my collection,
she announces. The other artists gasp.
Somewhere near the beach.
Artists all over the showroom
clap and cheer for her.

My father stands at the edge of the room,
claps his enormous hands
in rhythmic exhalation,
relief.

. . . .

I want this relief to find me too,
but all I can think about
is how much change is about to happen,
and I might not ever see the warehouse again.

Her Hands

On Thursday afternoons
after school,
my mom teaches drawing classes
at the Marin County Rec Center.
The best part is that Lisa
and her mom both go.

Lisa's the youngest student,
but my mom says she has a *real gift*.
She paints the entire canvas
without any fear. She just lets
the colors explode wherever she wants,
unafraid to get her hands dirty.

Sometimes we all get dinner after class,
and soon our moms become friends,
drink wine and talk
while me and Lisa write stories
and build worlds together.
She loves vintage music,
and I tell her about
the old TV shows and movies
I like to watch.

. . . .

Once after the drawing class,
Lisa, with her long, wild blond hair,
her hands full of charcoal and paint,
in her torn jeans, her Def Leppard T-shirt,
and her tall white boots,
took my hand and walked me outside.
What's it like having a mom like yours? she asked.
My mom drinks all the time, Ari.
All. The. Time. Even more after the divorce.

But all I could feel was her hand,
like it had stretched itself
over my whole body.
I didn't know how to answer
right away. I thought
about telling her what
I imagined she wanted to hear,
about art and studios
and books everywhere,
but being with her
made the truth just come out:
She smokes too much,
yells all the time,
and I never know
what will happen next.

I could see in her eyes
she was looking for something,
squeezing my hand tighter now,
like she might squeeze even more truth
out of me, a key to something.
I didn't know what to do.

but
    this hand
        in my hand

would unravel me.

Marzipan Potato

Sometimes after school, I skip
the first bus,
take the two-mile walk
home with Lisa.
    Just because.

    At the bakery
    Lisa shows me
    marzipan potatoes,
    a million calories
    of sugar, honey,
    and almond meal
    rolled into a potato-
    sized ball.

    On the walk,
    Lisa tells
    me about how
    her mom
    is having a really
    hard time,
    with her new boyfriend.
    They drink too much.

          . . . .

Plus, he is creepy,
always staring at me,
taking pictures of us.

We walk past
the Mill Valley
Lumberyard.
What about your dad?
I ask. She never talks about him.
We keep walking.
Lisa doesn't answer,
picks up a stone
and hurls it into the creek
along the side of the road.

I don't ask her again.

After the walk,
her mom isn't home.
Lisa invites me in.
She teaches me about
Def Leppard, her favorite band.
We play D&D,
write stories about faraway lands
that never existed
and the warriors who protected them.
In her stories,
women are always more powerful
than men.

What Happened on the Bike Path

They are coming for me.
    They hate me because
    they just do.
Oddball, fat kid, liar, show-off, and sometimes Jew.

pedal. pedal.
    handlebars. hold tight.
white egrets in the wind.
    space steady steady steady
calm, certain,
    still water
Pick, ahead of me.
    He's always faster.
It's not his fault. He is
    just trying to get away.
                I am too slow.

My body
too big
to move
the bike
out of
the way
in time.

Skin. Bone. Asphalt.

I made them crash,
they said.
I talk too much.
Kick my ass, huh?
Frank says, *Fatboy.*

....

    They come around me,
gather like reeds.
I stand. They back me off the bike path,
my feet in brackish water. Marsh grass
brushes my fingertips.

Pick looks over his shoulder
as he pedals away.
What is he supposed to do?

There is a moment
where I feel like
maybe I can beg
or even cry,
but I don't.

I let them do it to me.
I am fat. They always tell me this.
In the locker room. After school.
At the assembly just last week,
or birthday cupcakes in the classroom.
On the playground, picking teams at recess,
I guess
    I'll take
        Fatboy.

I don't belong. Too big to fit anywhere.
So I just stand there and let them do it to me.

I have always known the pain of being called names:
Fatboy,
Tubs,

Baby Huey—
and then Jewboy!
What's the matter, Jewboy?

I thought I knew about pain,
but I didn't know pain like this,
being punched so many times
that everything slows down,
the force of someone else's weight
being pushed into mine
over and over again.

stomach
shoulder
neck
hands pulling and twisting
legs pinched
fingers bent back

I feel the air pressed out of me
folded in half
fluttering like some injured bird
dirt and flying weeds
    and everything moving so fast
I can't keep them off me.
They keep coming,
inserting themselves
like long sticks from all directions
no way to time it,
to be ready,
    they poke
and push and punch
and still their words are coming

I can hear my own breath,
see blood on my jacket,
my bike, twisted
on the pavement.

Between breaths
I look in the distance for an adult,
someone who might
be able to stop all of this.

I think it's over   until   that last kick
        comes right into my stomach
the air squeezed out of me,
my head going back and back
down into the dirt,
until I can see him standing over me,
the great herons diving,
the muffled sound of bikes riding away

knowing that I'm not hurt bad enough to be dead
but knowing what death might feel like
if I just lay there long enough.

Somewhere in San Francisco
miles away from here
my parents are selling dresses
or looking at paintings.

I make it to Pick's house,

find the hidden key
beneath the loose board.
I thought Pick would be there,

but he's not.
I shower.
I put ice on my body.
I find a bed.
I hide the bruises.
    I hide them from everyone
inside all my extra skin.

Manhood

One night, my father talks
to me about my bar mitzvah.

It's about becoming a man, Ari,
taking responsibility,
standing up for yourself.

When he says this,
I almost find the courage
to tell him about what happened
on the bike path. But I don't
think he would understand.
After all, I didn't stand up
for myself, at least,
not the way he means.
He wants me to fight
back with fists.
I don't know if I want
to stand up for myself
in that way.
Why does being a man mean
I have to hurt someone else?

A long time ago
in Brooklyn,
at my grandparents' house,
we played tag
on the street outside
the brownstone.
In the middle of the game,
we stopped, something happened.
An older boy held a dragonfly
against the cement,
fingers pressed
on its thorax
and forewings.
It vibrated
beneath the sun.

Another older boy
held a magnifying glass
above its tail.
The lens collected the sun
from the asphalt.

The dragonfly searched
with 30,000 facets
of its compound eye
over the reaches of
its territory
its green wetland
a world away.

But then these older kids
crushed the dragonfly to the ground,

got on their bikes
and came after us instead.
They took our toys,
pushed us down,
even pulled the girls' hair.

We went upstairs
to tell the fathers.
My father took
a long wooden spoon
from the kitchen,
put it into my palm.
Here, he said,
    stick this in his spokes.

We went back
armed with spoons and dowels,
golf clubs and two umbrellas,
and we thrust them into the spokes
of the tires
like pistons firing
into wiry chaos
until we got one.
But in that moment
I didn't feel like a man at all.
I felt   cruel.

The first kid flew
over his handlebars,
his arms tucked under him,
his shoulders
sudden and forward,
his face, pale, ageless,

skidded across the concrete
from knee, to shoulder, to head,
his own blood pooling
around his hands,
one leg up, turned
toward the sky.

Legs and bikes
and long hair
and smashed dragonfly wings.

 Kids.
Not enemies,
not friends.
 Kids
who made mistakes,
who could not turn
one bloody cheek for another.

I don't want to go through that again.
There has to be a different way
to stand up for myself,
to take responsibility,
to be a man.

How to Appear Less Fat
According to my mom's fashion magazine

One)
Shoulders back and up,
butt directly under,
chin turned down,

head slightly forward
to avoid double chin.
Arch lower back slightly.
This will cause the stomach to elongate
just enough to avoid
    "rolling."
This will also ease tension on
any button, belt, or zipper
or any combination of these.
Breathe shallow,
short and through the nose,
mouth closed and grave.
Smiles are for later.
Be sure that the lower back
does not touch the back of the chair.
Avoid any chance of indentation,
unless when sitting in the back
of the room,
then slouching is okay.
Nobody is watching you.
Nobody is thinking of this.
But *you* are.
You are.

Two)
An exercise to get rid of
a double chin.

An extra chin
lives with me.
It's part of my neck
and my head
and it won't go away.

Sometimes I imagine
my headaches
come from the weight
pulling my head down
all day.
Twice a day,
I lean my head back
whenever I can
stretch the skin
from chest to chin.
I lift it up
elongate and count to ten,
twice a day.
This will work
if I stay with it.

Elevate, Arise, Walk Home

Baruch a ta Adonai
El-u hey . . . arggghh!
I get it wrong every time,
and I cry a little
from frustration.
Did you practice?
the rabbi asks.
Yeesss! I lie.

The rabbi sits patiently
in his overstuffed chair.
He drones the blessings
back to me. We start again.

. . . .

His office smells like honey
and pipe tobacco and books.
He shines at me from beneath
the one lamp that he allows.

I want to break out of here,
but I like him, even though
he is tough. *Again, Ari.*
Elevate. What? You don't
want to make your parents proud?

I do.
But what I really want
is to jump on my bike,
ride through Chrissy Field
all the way to Fort Point
and the Golden Gate.
I want to feel my legs
burn from riding.
I want a Three Musketeers.

Here, he says,
let's record today.
And he fumbles
with an old tape recorder,
hits Record and Play
at the same time.

In a few months,
I will receive my aliyah,
being called to the Torah.
My bar mitzvah,
where the rabbi

will call me up,
tell me to *Arise*
in front of his congregation
and recite blessings
and prayers.
When it's all done,
according to tradition,
I become a man.

But I don't know if this can work.
My dad says we are lucky
to find a rabbi who would
still help us.
Most kids start years before.
They attend Hebrew school,
or even take classes online,
but my parents
always seemed too busy
to get it going.
Part of me hoped
they might even forget.

The more I learn
about these traditions,
how important they are,
how intricate,
the more nervous I get.
After it's done,
I need to observe all 613 mitzvot,
feeding the poor,
being kind to strangers,
honoring my parents—
so much responsibility.

I remember my cousin's
bat mitzvah,
rhythmic prayers,
and unending songs,
and grown-up tears,
but mostly I remember
my cousin,
radiant in her
cream-colored dress,
her eyes
filled with blue and white,
a sudden and beautiful woman.

Bright moonlight
and party lights,
fireflies in the grass,
dancing in strobe lights,
with cousins and friends
deep into the night.
Games: Hula-Hoop
and hot potato,
a thousand dance contests,
Coke and Pepsi.

Brisket, chopped liver,
baskets of bread
and chocolate rugelach,
near a counter filled
with black-and-white cookies.

My aunt Cookie
and my grandparents

at the long cedar table
near the pond.
The fireflies rose
and doubled on the water.
The grown-ups spent the evening there,
speaking a secret language of hope
and memory.
They stopped each time
a child passed
to smile or pat a head,
adjust a tie,
wipe a mouth.

I found my mother and father
dancing, his left hand
straight out, holding her hand tightly.
They were looking at each other
in a black tuxedo and a silver gown
and the starlight.

Later that night, I ask them if mine will be like this.
Better! my father says, and he grabs my face.
Better, you mensch.

Again, Ari, the rabbi says,
and I start again.

June

Clothes Like Spider-Man

I always wanted
to look like Peter Parker,
just a kid, like me,
trying to figure it all out.
The clothes seem
to just hang off his body,
like he doesn't need them at all.

For a while,
I wore a vest
like Han Solo's.
I liked the way it covered my belly.

At Camp Shalom,
near the lake,
I used to watch everyone else,

shirts off, their bodies
tight-skinned and unashamed.
I wanted to be able to do that,
to just stand there in myself.

I want to be like Mark,
broad-shouldered
and muscle-armed.
His 501s in perfect form,
tight around the waist,
the Levi's patch on display,
32/30, lightly wrinkled at the knee,
a perfect fold at the foot.

On the bike path,
when Frank kicked my leg
while I lay on the ground,
my shirt had crept up
over my stomach and back
from the fall off the bike.
The fly on my own
501s was unbuttoned;
I never button it when I ride,
too tight, too uncomfortable.
They laughed at the way
my belly filled the open space.
I might have laughed too
if I were standing there,
my 501s, 40/32.

Spider-Man's suit
is skintight,

and that must feel weird.
At least, though,
he gets to wear a mask.

Who Am I?

In our San Francisco apartment,
Pick and I wait for my mom
to take us out to Stinson Beach,
where we will spend the summer.
Pick's mom says he can stay over as much as possible.

We stack our backpacks
and fill a wide green
cardboard box
with books and markers
and drawing pads
for the game
we are designing.

Flip-flops and swim trunks,
flashlights and first-aid kits,
his old iPad for recording,
robot action figures strictly
for reference for the robots
in the game.

Dice, lead figures,
folders full of graph paper.
We pack our "survival" knives
we bought at the flea market,

complete with compass in the hilt.
Pick's stack of vintage records:
the Cars, Prince, Van Halen,
Duran Duran, the Police,
Michael Jackson, Madonna.

Books: *1984*; *Ogre, Ogre*; Harry Potter books;
Dune; *The Hunger Games*;
a bunch of graphic novels;
and of course
my favorite book,
the bible of cryptozoology
and supernatural stuff,
the hardback edition
of *Arthur C. Clarke's*
Mysterious World.

Pick carefully packs
his *Robotech RPG* sourcebooks
into his game folders
and then suddenly asks,
So, did you tell your
parents about what happened
on the bike path?

Of course.
      I look away.

      actually   *no.*

I can feel Pick is annoyed.
His voice suddenly fills the hallway:

What's wrong with you?
Why are you hiding it?
It's like you stuff down
every bad thing that happens
like you stuff down pizza at lunch.

I look at him.
    He takes a breath.

Sorry, Ari, I didn't mean that,
it's just . . .
    I look down at the floor.
No, you're right, I say.
They'll just get mad at me.
He'll want me to fight back.
It'll make things even worse.
That's usually what happens
to me anyway.

Things get worse.

I shrink even as I pull up my pants.
The elastic wears out so quickly
and the pants always fall just below
my belly line.

    I turn myself toward him.
His face straightens,
taller now, stronger.
He moves his hands up and down
in frustration, like no matter what
he says, I won't listen.
Argh! You are such a coward, Ari.

I am.

But he doesn't stop. He says
words and phrases: *overweight, grow up.*
Then he kicks his backpack over.
Stop feeling sorry for yourself! he shouts.

Words spin into webs, filling the apartment
with silken memories of things I said,
and memories of late-night talks
about how I look, and how much I wish
I could change, mixed with
promises unfulfilled: The trip we never took,
video games unplayed, histories confused.
I am completely tangled up.
Sometimes, Ari, it's so hard to be your friend.
You stay with us,
you say you want help,
but you don't tell us what's going on with you.
You say you want to change,
but you are too busy feeling sorry for yourself!

His voice gets louder and louder, and then suddenly
trails off into quiet words:
Who do you think you are?

His words, finally, feel like a slap across my face,
and suddenly my fists clench.

Who am I? I yell back, my words echoing
in the hall, a defense, a learned movement
taken from my parents,

a higher pitch blown back at a defensive angle,
but hollow and with no teeth.
And in my mind, I ask myself,
Yeah, who am I?

My name is Ari Rosensweig.
Last year, I was the newest kid
at school.
I am a fat kid, and I hate it
when people call me *Fatboy*.
My life doesn't feel good enough,
and I don't know how to change it.

I start to make a story of defense in my head,
to answer the question of who I am
in one mighty sentence
or even to make another layer
of promise about getting revenge
for what happened on the bike path,
but Pick knows me too well. He knows
that I don't want to fight.

Look, Ari. You always tell me
I am like your brother. Trust me.
I think we can make some changes.
I want to trust him,
like he's my real brother.
He is trying to help me, I think.
He's asking me what I am going to do about it.

Things calm down,
and we start talking about
the ways that the robots

in our game might adapt
to beach conditions.

By the end of the morning,
his words are at work,
and I feel that this summer
is already something else
than what I thought it would be,
not the end of seventh grade,
but the start of a new story
all my own.

The Nursery

My mother stops
at the first left
off Shoreline Highway
in Stinson Beach.

It's an old, broken-down plant nursery,
a big gravel parking lot
with light-pink stones.

Vines grow wild over old
wooden fence posts
and rusting wire.
This is a place that could be anything.

We walk in slowly.
The place is open to the sky in every direction,
salt and wet air,
corroded terraces

covered with cracked plastic sheeting
and piles of collected driftwood,
ornamental and smooth.
A kitchen, bathroom with an old mirror,
and lots of tiny rooms for planting
and storage and everything else.

Space.

My mother walks to the center of the courtyard
and spins. She actually spins.
She does this in moments where things come together.
This, she says, *is ours.*
Ours. I say it to myself.
We look at each other,
unsure.
We can actually hear the waves crashing down the beach,
the real and the dream, like so much sand and water.

Inside

There are shelves in the main room for display,
an old kitchen,
several workrooms,
alcoves, a broken kiln,
plastic bags of molded soil.
All the rooms
face the courtyard
in a giant horseshoe.

Dirt everywhere,
spread across the floors,

broken wood railings,
and cracked concrete,
an old walkway
between growing things,
vines reaching
and flowers sprouting,
the ground left to its own.

In the middle of the courtyard
is a plant graveyard,
organic matter dried to black.
A mulch pile, smelly, worm-filled.
I climb to the top
and stomp down a conquering foot.

This is the place
where my mother will escape,
reclaim her artist self,
and take me with her.

Who am I? I think, Pick's question
still burning in my chest.
This question, like me,
too big to be asked
or answered in words.

Digging in the Dirt

A marine layer
sits on top of everything,
washing the wood.
More cleaning today.

Mom moves boxes,
pedestals, containers,
and paint.
I haul boxes of brushes
from car to studio,
sponges and rounds,
filberts and fans,
mops and riggers,
horsehair and synthetic
mixed together.

Pick and I clear the mulch pile,
sorting the larger debris,
random leaves and cuttings.
The smell is noxious, overwhelming.
Chemicals release,
mix with saltwater air,
organic things,
beautiful things,
breaking down.

Even solid things like buildings can change,
sometimes corrode when they are not cared for.

By the time the sun is overhead,
my arms are sore, tired, scratched,
my legs chafed red,
but it feels good.

We do this for hours,
slowly at times,
until the last piece of rot
is undone and pushed away.

Trolls

On Sunday, my mother
cuts the ends of a clay brick,
gives me and Pick
each a half brick,
a bowl of water,
wire-threaded sticks,
and a wooden spoon.
Use this—she points
to the edge of some chrome tool—
for the finer points.

Pick makes
simple, definable creatures.
At first it seems that they're
from the game we are creating,
but soon I can tell they're
trolls or gnomes of some kind,
big as thumbs.
Some have hats that actually can come off.
Some have weapons
    or pets.
I make one,
green and tall,
with a long staff,
and another, its
belly falling over its waist.

He fills a tray with the creatures,
a metal baking sheet
where the trolls are clamoring
to make their way off,

to maybe slip into the dark places
of the gallery.

We take them to burn in the round
kiln in the courtyard.

When they are finished
and airing in the sun,
we paint the trolls
different colors,
sloppy at first, but we get better.
Pick puts tiny
price tags on their feet,
then hides them around the gallery.
Later on, some kids will find
one and pull it down in wonder,
carrying it
two-handed to some
wandering grown-up.
When one sells, we call it
going home.
We make a clay box the size of a big fist,
and trolls crawl all over it.
We put money in the box
every time
a troll goes home.

Sunday Drive

By the next Sunday,
my father visits,
and he puts us

in the back of the Sunbird.
The wind is blowing my head off.
My father drives with the top down.
   Always.
He wears Porsche sunglasses
and a long coat
with a million pockets.
He was made for this.
But my insides are a step behind
each twist and turn.
He traces the lines
of the winding roads
and me and Pick hang on
until it's over.
  My father comes on Sundays, sometimes.
     Doesn't stay long.

A Talk in the Car

Mom loves to take drives too,
in an old yellow four-door truck
she bought to haul her creations.
We learn how to handle
the winding roads.
I listen to my mother talk
about a million ideas
she has for the nursery.
I think she thinks I'm an adult.
I learn to listen.

Somewhere
between Muir Woods

and Stinson,
where the road winds
and is full of disaster,
Pick asleep in the back,
she starts to talk about my father.
When I met him, you know, he was so handsome.
And then some details about suits
and hairstyles, Hawaii, crashing a dune buggy,
riding horses.

Today, just before the Bolinas Lagoon
spills blue from behind the mountain,
   as I am lost in my own thoughts,
she says,
    He was incredible at lovemaking.
Her accent suddenly flares,
almost unrecognizable,
thrown back into a Bronx summer.
I don't look. I just stare at the window.
I wonder what would happen
if I opened the door and rolled
out of the car?

What about you?
Do you ever, you know?

It feels like she read a book
or watched a TV show
that told her to "talk to your kid."
I say nothing, look toward the Pacific.
I grip my seat belt.
I want to tell her what I'm going through,
that the changes in my body terrify me,

that I'm seeing myself in the mirror
and I feel so much weight,
that I'm filled up,
sometimes with sadness,
sometimes with hate.

I want to tell her that I lie all the time
so people will like me.
I lie to myself about why I'm this way.
I want to tell her that everything is changing.
I want to tell her that I don't understand
anything I'm going through,
and that my mind has a mind of its own.

We roll straight into town,
turn left into the nursery,
the quiet crackling of gravel
beneath slow-moving rubber tires,
and she waits, looking at me.
If I could, I would just let her see
inside my mind because I don't know
how to tell her,
         so instead I just say,
I'm fine.

Fat at the Beach

At the beach,
boogie boards and sand shovels,
shirts and sandals
and towels in a heap,
and everyone runs to the water,

the sand kicked under heels.
I feel the way my body flops.
The freckled girl looks over,
runs next to me,
stares, points,
and says, *Fat*.

When I hear them say *fat*, I feel

    naked

completely uncomfortable.

I slip,
fall back,
the front
of my black shirt
rolls up
my stomach,
exposed
fat,
the ribs
tucked inside
undulating rolls
of fleshy whale skin.
Silence lingers
in the sand.

It's the stark,
sudden loneliness,
the no-pants dream
made real.

It seems to matter more now
than ever before,
a weight on my body
like a friend suddenly cruel,
like a bad word whispered
in a library aisle,
stupid, moron,
or the first punch
in my gut where I can't
find my breath.

This new feeling,
a sudden and irrevocable
change because of a word
and a look
and a lifetime
of a feeling
that I never understood
until now,
where everyone else is perfect
and my life is different
because someone called me fat
and I am.

The Game

Pick and I
focus a lot on our game.
We started making it last year,
a new role-playing game

about the future:
    charts and dice and drawings,
    giant robots bigger than the Golden Gate
    rise out of the ocean
    to protect San Francisco.

We script the first aliens ever discovered,
life-forms, brilliant engineers
who talk to machines with their minds,
merge with humans,
eat radiation.

We fill walls with graph paper,
hinge the edges together
in tape and glue.
We calculate probabilities and probability curves,
argue about how-many-sided dice we need.

We structure character generation,
attributes, debate
the importance of charisma,
invent heroes,
plot cities and space stations
and underwater domes,
storyline after storyline
between humans, creatures, robots, and monsters.

We place a *Dungeon Master's Guide*
in the center of wherever we work,
our inspiration, a shrine to Gary Gygax
one of the creators of the original
Dungeons & Dragons.

In school
we learned
to make a plan,
write it down,
so the work is real.
We linger in twilight
before the sun rises,
two boys with the world
in front of them,
making a choice
to be like brothers.

Pizza

Friday evening,
the lights in the town come on
in a slow flicker.
Families walk here to there for dinner,
and we watch the world happen
from behind the nursery fence,
rusted wire and rotted wood.
Pick and I notice
how many kids there are,
                    girls our age.

Near the nursery
there is a pizza place like a barn,
and we convince my mother to take us
the one hundred steps and buy us dinner.

Inside, the room is stuffed
like a breath being held,
the air is basil and pesto and bread.
We order an extra-large,
laugh about the day.
At the table,
we pull clay from our pockets
and sculpt tiny trolls.
Each one holds
the Parmesan or the red pepper,
a fork like a pike, a spoon
as a tiny bed.

When the pizza comes,
    it's perfect.
Pizza is made of magic.
Perfect cheese, perfect sauce,
and perfect crust, perfect smell,
perfect.
I down my first piece before
anyone else's second bite.
I feel myself eyeing the slices,
counting them,
worried that I won't get enough.
I need to make sure I do, so I eat fast.
Another. And more like this, until
I find that I have eaten half the pie.

Slow
    down, my mother says sharply.
She shakes her head at me.
She's seen this too many times.

....

I want to,
but I don't.

Once, my aunt Cookie told me
I should wait for my mind
to catch up with my stomach.

The moon is out now.
The waves crash and disappear
in the distance.
We play around,
running from car to car,
ducking in and out,
some tag or battle game.
We decide to launch
a race for the last fifty steps
back to the gallery.
Pick blows past me
and through groups of people
walking around the town.
Then, out of nowhere,
I hear the sudden voice
of some young man,
a group just passing by,
as my heavy legs reach Pick's dust cloud
swirling in the moonlight

You'll get 'em next time, Fatboy,

and then laughter in the dark
from somewhere in the space
I just ran past.

....

Pick is in the nursery now,
already putting his pizza troll
on the shelf.

When You Are Fat . . .

there are
long stretches
when you don't
think about
the way your body presses
against your clothes,
when you don't feel tired
when you run in the sun
like everyone else.

There are times
when you eat dinner
and nobody
looks at you funny,
like you might eat
way more than your share.

There are times
that you can just be
who you are.

There are also times
when your body betrays you.
There are times
when you feel
like you can't stop eating,

because eating
is the only way
you know
how to

     feel

                    right

                              again.

Something Finally Happened

That night, we sleep
on our old camping mats
in the planting room,
our sleeping bags
zipped over our heads.
Outside, the cold marine layer
settles over the town,
the buildings submerged
in wet summer fog.

I half dream all night
about voices in the dark
like a choir singing out
a million mean names
through my life,
piling on top of me
like old blankets.
When my eyes finally open,
I feel the weight still on me.
My hands move to my belly.

Too soft, I think.
Too much.

I remember a doctor's visit in fifth grade.
The doctor talked about salad,
told me to try Italian dressing.
It makes the green stuff good.
Once a day, he said. *A salad.*

I tiptoe through
the nursery,
across the creaking wood,
trying not to wake everyone.
The door to the nursery bathroom
is a barn door that locks.
I lay a piece of wood into
the brackets, but the wood
is loose and spaced.
I hang a towel on the door
for more privacy.

I stand in the bathroom
in front of the old brass mirror.
It's warped across the center,
creates illusions,
widens anyone in its frame.

I'm certain that they can hear me looking at myself.

I stare in the mirror,
and I don't see what I want to see.

....

I like myself, sometimes,
but it feels like the person
in the mirror isn't me anymore.

I stare,
close my eyes,
remember . . .

a New York schoolyard.
The dodgeball
hits me squarely
in the chest.
I fall back.
My shirt pulls up,
and the innocent laughter
of other kids
and my own laughter
to cover it all up.

> Or my father, at a fancy dinner,
> before he says anything else, introduces
> me to his business partner as *husky.*

I tell people I'm *naturally a bigger person.*

The mirror is slightly tilted.
That's why I look this way. I tell myself
the mirror is tilted and warped.
Then I catch myself.

I grab the sink,
hold tight.

I won't let myself lie.
Not now.
    No lie.
        Not now.

I hear my mother and Pick
moving in the gallery,
the sounds of morning conversations,
cereal boxes and fruit bowls.

I let go of the sink,
slide my hands to my sides,
grab my love handles
where they spill
over my pajama pants.

I can't stop looking at my body,

and for the first time, the way I look
becomes me
all the way.

I feel horrible. Heavy.
Stagnant water in a bucket.

In seventh grade
we learned about heavy water.
Regular water has a single proton
in each nucleus of its hydrogen atom.
In heavy water, each hydrogen atom
has a neutron too.
Neutrons, unstable, lonely,

do everything they can to stick to the proton,
make the water more dense, heavy.
My body is filled with heavy water.

Unstable, I place my hands
around my love handles
and get a good, strong grip,
sandwich the flesh between
my thumb and fingers
until my fat fills my palms.

Why does it have to be like this?
Most people will tell me that it's my fault.

I want to feel something other
than sorry for myself.
I tighten my grip,
and even as I do, I hear
Pick's voice saying
he wants to help me,
and for a moment
I think about getting help,

but I don't. Instead, in the wet air,
in the quiet,
I just
        squeeze.

I squeeze,
        feeling the thumbs
        dig into my body.
Press,
        press.

It hurts.
I let up a bit.
My sides throb in redness,
my fingers flushed
and pushed in,
and already
    a small amount
        of blood.

I think about Pick saying,
Who are you?
I think of the night before and the voice of the
    stranger.
    Get 'em next time, Fatboy.
I remember more now,
images of jeans too tight
and shirts poking out in weird places
and names that I must have pushed far away.
    I remember New York
    and the grandparents always declaring
    how skinny my cousins are.

I think about how
this is summer,
and we are at the beach.
And everyone sees me as fat.

Teeth gritting,
I feel it like a burn,
my hands to my sides,
the thumbnails now
pushing down
on the same spot

        push
              press

until the ache is overwhelming.
I feel the control of it,
the pain
working its way into my blood.

I watch myself do this
in the old mirror.
        press
              my face sweating

                            skin pale

I do this
        until the blood comes
              over my fingernails,
and I don't stop
until it hurts so much
I scream.

I hear the others hearing me.
I want them to.

I squeeze harder.
        press
              push
                    squeeze
I feel my face flush with tears
that fill my eyes until
the mirror fades into mist,
the sky dark.

                    . . . .

I am falling,
I think,
falling down.

I feel my shirtless body scrape
along the wood door,
I feel the sudden relief of pain stopping.

Sometime later,
I open my eyes
and I am on
top of my sleeping bag.
I see Pick sitting by the counter.
My mother is holding my hand,
and her face is wet with tears.
I feel an ache in my sides.
When I look down, I see
the pain has turned purple.
What happened? I ask.

My mother looks at me,
grips my hand.
    She doesn't answer.

Doctor

Sometime after *the incident,*
as my mother now refers to it,
she takes me to the doctor,
a psychiatrist.
We drop off Pick,

make plans to see him soon,
and drive from Marin
back to San Francisco.

The car is silent the rest of the way.
I don't know what to say,
but she tries to fill the quiet
with plans and questions.

We are going on a diet,
she says. *It's time,* she says.
She tells me about
how she used to take a pill,
no bigger than a pin,
that kept her
from getting hungry,
kept her awake,
helped her *see things*
in a whole new way.
I painted all night, she says.
I don't even remember how it happened.
She tells me about
filling galleries
with paintings,
department stores
with hand-painted dresses.

But first, she says,
we need to talk about what happened.
We climb up and down
San Francisco streets
until we get there.

....

The doctor's office
is like an apartment.
We wait in stinky chairs,
watch two little boys
destroy a puzzle,
their mom deep
in the world of her phone.

The doctor is kind and old.
He says my whole name,
Ari . . . Samuel . . . Rosensweig,
asks me if I like my name.
I don't know? Yes?
At first I don't like
his one-sided voice,
the words coming
out of just the left side.
He talks to me about school,
asks me questions about girls.
I don't really know what to say.

He expects something from me.
He asks me directly about what happened,
and I feel my side ache.
You know, Ari, sometimes
we harm ourselves
because we don't know
what else to do.

I stare at him.

I think I need to talk about this.

My thoughts and my words
swirl around, and I'm not sure
if I'm thinking or speaking.
I start talking about feeling distracted,
about how my body
seems like a different place
than it's ever been,
like sometimes it's on fire.

He seems good at listening.

Finally, he asks
if my mother
will leave.

When she does,
the doctor smiles,
asks me about *puberty*.
I fold my arms across my body,
look at the books on the shelf.
I want to say
I don't know anything,
but I think about the time
when I was eight,
and tell him about when
my friends and me
saw something on the computer
we shouldn't have seen.
We acted like
we understood
the confusing scenes,
the awful voices,

the inhuman sounds.
    We all felt sick.

I tell the doctor that
it doesn't feel like that anymore,
that it just makes me scared.

I feel like he is actually listening.

Somehow this doctor knows my questions
Without me even asking them.
One by one,
he tells me things I need to hear,
lights turning on,
pieces of puzzles
that seemed lost
suddenly fitting into
unexpected places.
Sometimes, he says,
*you may feel afraid when lots
of changes happen
in your home environment.
It's normal to feel this way, Ari.*

At the end
of the hour,
he settles deep into his chair,
smiles, and takes a long breath.
So, he says.

Will you tell me what happened in the bathroom?
. . . .

I don't know. I look down,
pull my socks up higher.
It won't happen again, I say.
He looks at me,
smiles.
It won't, I say.
He puts an unexpected hand
on my shoulder.

Apartment Doctor

I convince my mom
I don't need
to go to the apartment doctor again,
even though he helped me.

I should have gone back.

It's just that
I don't want
to think about
what happened
or talk it over.
I wish I could take
the memory,
throw it into the bay,
watch it slowly sink
into the salt water,
down and down,
washed away forever
into the cold darkness.

Another Kind of Doctor

The paper
on this doctor's table
crumples beneath
my weight.
Food pyramids
cover the walls,
mostly green,
the vegetables and fruits
delicious in the posters.
Deep-red apples
where the bite taken out
is white like cartoon apples.
The broccoli pleads
with giant eyes
to be eaten two to four times daily.
There are dancing grapes
and carrot sticks
and breads pushed to the back,
near a lonely triangle
of forgotten pizza.

The doctor comes in.
His skin is made
of glossy magazine pages
and his hair is brown paper.
    He has me step on the scale.
    He has me stand against the wall.
    He has me try to touch my toes.
From this position,
he takes an instrument
like thin pliers

and presses them gently
to my sides. Cold, I flinch,
not from the pain
but from the memory of the pain.
When he sees the sores,
deep purple and black,
his breathing changes,
and he whispers
in a doctor's voice,
How did this happen?

I answer by holding up my hands,
pushing my thumbs into my fingertips.
He nods.

He is careful to avoid
the sores,
the huge purple bruises.

He moves me from the bench to a chair,
goes to a drawer,
removes a package
of folded papers,
some glossy plastic and cardboard wheels,
and other packages full of colors.

He asks my mom into the room
and for the next thirty minutes
she nods and writes stuff down.
The doctor spins the wheel,
which is actually five wheels,
each a different color,
talks about points,

and colors meaning points,
and points meaning gaining
or losing weight.
He talks about targets
and colors that are pie pieces.
Spins the wheels
in different directions
to where a whole pie
filled with mostly green slices
sits at the center.

Thirty pounds, he says.
I need you to lose at least thirty pounds.

I hold the wheel, spin the different sections.
It smells like paint
and plastic,
a mutated rainbow,
an impossible request.
My arms out,
he fills them up with posters
and a button with the mutated rainbow on it.

On the way to the nursery,
my mother hatches plans.
We'll buy a juicer, she says.

Broken Promise

We never buy a juicer.

The Answer?

She stands over the bed,
cradles a book in her arms,
rocks it like a baby.
I have it, she says. *I've got it.*
She holds up a yellow book.
There's a man in a suit on the cover
sitting at a desk.
I knew this doctor in the sixties
in New York. I did a portrait
of his wife.

This doctor wrote a diet book!
It really works!

She uncradles the book,
looks at the cover,
and spins it onto the bed.

I lift it,
hold it in both hands,
feel the compact weight
of the book.

When my feet hit the floor,
she explains how it works.
She talks about carbohydrates
and how evil sugar is.
The more she tells me
the more I realize that this diet
isn't like any other.

. . . .

It's the end of bread,
potato chips, cookies,
cereal, and even pizza.

But maybe it's a chance for real change.

We Need to Get Lisa

The next morning, starving,
I walk into the kitchen. My mother is
muttering, tapping furious
texts on her phone.

Something's happened. We need to get Lisa.
I remember the quiver of Lisa's voice
when she told me about her mom.

I unwrap a piece
of cheese,
open *Mysterious World*,
nervously read about Bigfoot.

We need to get her, my mother mutters again.
She may need to stay with us for a while.

I think about Lisa.

1. She looks like a superhero in the comics
    we read.
2. She's kind.
3. She plays Dungeons & Dragons with me.
4. She's an amazing artist.

5. She writes stories.
6. She likes me for who I am.
7. She punched Rick Casterol in the nose when
   he said something he shouldn't have.
8. She always sticks up for me.

I fold the book down onto the table.
My mother paces back and forth,
then suddenly stops
and looks me in the eyes.
Something's happened, Ari.
Lisa's mom needs to go away
for a little while. She's sick,
and she needs time to get well.

On Our Way

We pass Shoreline Highway,
our usual route onto Miller Avenue,
the bike path on my right,
the one I ride from the Dolan house,
from Pick's house.

I watch for snowy egrets
in the fog,
and in the distance
I see the middle school
on my left.

I unwrap another cheese stick,
imagine the faces of classmates.
I picture the first day of next year,

walking on campus,
the lighter steps,
the better clothes,
the hope of feeling more free.
I watch myself walking
up the stairs before the first bell,
no one staring.
No extra layers of me,
just another boy.

Sometimes the silence of others
is better than attention.

Twenty-Three Steps

We pass the depot
in the heart of downtown,
turn on
Throckmorton Avenue
toward Old Mill Park.
On the right are the long
stone steps of Lisa's house.

Twenty-three steps.
I count them every time.
Wait here, my mother says.
I wait in the car,
shift in my clothes,
working to find comfort.
My shorts feel tight,
and l lift my legs slightly up
so that fat doesn't spread

on the seat.
I hate how it looks.

Lisa meets her halfway
down the steps,
blue dress cut low, white sandals,
her blond hair wet
from a shower.

In my chest, I feel the excitement
of seeing my friend,
but also I feel fire
in my body,
and I don't know how to put it out.

She hugs my mother
until she folds,
her face pressed into
my mother's shoulder.
They stand together on the stairs
for a long time.
My mother is talking to her.
Lisa is nodding,
her eyes full and wet.
I watch them until
she looks toward me, and I see
an unexpected little girl, quiet.

I put Def Leppard on the radio,
turn it way up,
roll the window down
enough for her to hear.
Joe Elliott sings "Photograph."

I make it louder.
She smiles
just a little.

Silly

I let her ride in the front seat.
When we pass Muir Woods,
my mother talks to us about
redwoods, but we are
busy saying *Muir*
over and over,
lengthening it . . .
mmuuuuiiirrr, meeeeuuuuuiiirrr
until finally,
mannurrree.
She smiles. We laugh.
Kids again.

A Tour

When we get there,
we run from one end to the other,
my voice racing
to explain every nuance,
the driftwood piles,
wooden spool tables,
the studios in the back,
the archery range Pick
and I put in the mulch pile,
and the bows we made.

She picks one up and fires an arrow.
Me and Pick worked hard
on this. He's a good shot.
He can show you when
he gets here. She smiles.

Let me show you the trolls!
On the way
she stops,
stares at a sculpture
of a giant woman,
her eyes wild,
and there are figures coming out of her hair,
their tiny clay hands
on the woman's neck.

The longer Lisa looks,
the more she sees.

I walk to her and set down
one of the trolls we made
holding a tiny wood sign
that reads THIS WAY TO THE BEACH
while he flexes a tiny troll muscle.

But she just stares into the eyes of the sculpture.
Meet Melinda, I say.
Then in a low voice I mutter, *Creepy.*
She laughs, then looks across the road
and up toward the mountain.
We should climb to those trees, she says,
and points to a forest near the highest peak,
where the Dipsea Trail cuts over

the mountains.
Yeah, we should, I say.
Lisa takes me by the hand.
Show me where you make the trolls.

Breakfast

I

I wait at the table in the garden
for Lisa to wake up,
so we can go to breakfast.
I sit near *Melinda,*
my mother's creation,
an eight-foot-tall
terra-cotta sculpture.
She leans forward.
One clay hand reaches
for the sun.
The other presses the earth.
One foot is forward,
the other placed firmly
along a metal armature.

One day, a magazine will come
and write a story about
what a feat this sculpture is,
how each section
was fired separately in the kiln,
about glue and hoses,
metal bars and pipe threads,
about movements in art,
about rising and falling.

For now, *Melinda*
watches me
waiting for Lisa.

Lisa walks into the garden,
makes a face at *Melinda*,
and sits down, her hands in the pocket
of her gray hoodie.

II
At the Coast Bar and Grill,
my mother explains
the diet,
and Lisa tries to take it in.
We order bacon and eggs
with extra bacon.
We order a side of cheese.

Sometimes it's just easier
to show someone how this all works.

When the food comes,
Lisa is eating her blueberry pancakes
with a river of syrup.
My mother puts her arm around me,
smiles to comfort
me away from the smell of the syrup,
and without thinking,
she slides her hands down to my love handles,
a normal, loving gesture.
She turns to Lisa,
We're going to work on this mensch,

. . . .

and she squeezes.

She's forgotten the wound.
I cry out
because it still hurts.
I pull the linen napkin
over my mouth.
She remembers right away,
takes her hands off.
I feel her body stiffen.
I feel weak,
but I feel something else too,
that things have to be different,
that I need to change.
The names, the pokes, the looks
pile in every glass and jar,
cup and bowl
in the restaurant,
and at last I feel
the weight of my body.
Too heavy to be me.

In the middle of the restaurant,
I spill tears into my breakfast,
aware that there is no promise,
no magic pill, no work
except my work.
I make fists
in the tablecloth,
whisper
quiet prayers,
Please help.

Before the Opening

Mom says
today is about work,
because tonight is about
the opening,
for the world to see
the nursery-turned-gallery.

Pick's mom drops him off
to stay for a few days.
Just in time for the work! I say.
Did you show Lisa everything? he asks,
and we run around the nursery,
everything new again
until we hear the yell
to get to work.

We walk from corner to corner,
pick up broken arrows,
dried clay, water balloon
shreds, and everything else.
We rake piles of
ashen leaves, and our breath
fills with dust.

We carry paintings two by two,
stretch canvases across
wood beams,
hang metal wires
and awkward hooks.
We swing on ladders
and go on the roof.

Pick carries in a new shipment of clay
bag by bag.
Lisa folds linens with my mother,
helps to paint new tiles.
My mother is teaching her brushstrokes,
hatching, scrambling, glazing.
Lisa is a good student.

My mother has been changing since
the morning, and by two p.m. she is
completely transformed into the Artist.
She holds a brush in one hand
and a glass of champagne full of grapes in the other.
She is painting the air with directions,
calling out commands
until our ears break.

Lisa and Pick string white Christmas lights
across the beams above the patio.
My mother sets out the wine and the champagne,
the cheese boards, bowls of almonds and olives.
Is your dad coming? Pick asks.
No, I say,
but I don't really know.

— The Opening

People flow into the nursery,
some to look at art,
some to meet the eccentric

Artist from the city,
some to drink free wine.

When the crowd dies down a little,
we sit on the roof,
beneath the beach stars,
watch the Artist come and go
while people talk, eat cheese,
and stare in front of sculptures,
nod in front of paintings.

People can really stare
at a painting for a long time,
Pick says.
Lisa laughs. *That's how you're*
supposed to look at art.
She points down to where
an older woman stands
by a painting of Icarus
staring out across the wide sea,
her eyes filled with tears.

See, Lisa says.
First you look at the scene,
let it hit you
however it does.
Then you look
at one thing at a time,
try to see each figure,
each shape and how it's made.
Streaks of color,
hard strokes or washes,

the way the figures
in the painting
connect or don't.
I look at her
examining the painting,
her face beaming with joy.
She's where she's supposed to be,
and I get to be here too.
We see a few people who want to buy trolls,
and we jump down from the roof
to help the trolls *go home.*

At the end of the night, my mom
rests in the tall peacock chair.
The first of many! she says.

It takes us the whole next day to clean it all up.

Night in the Nursery

We all sleep
in one of the old planting rooms.
It's big enough for each
of us to have plenty of space,
high beams
and a skylight in the center.
Sunlight and moonlight
fill the room.
We make it ours for the summer.
We paint the slatted walls
with heavy acrylic,

blues, greens, yellows, and browns,
smoothed into river mud,
a thick-pasted canvas.

We hang our drawings of robots,
landscapes, and cartoon trolls,
animated versions of the sculptures,
the *Lotus Keeper*, the *Ice Priest*,
surfing in the waves
or climbing into the hills.
I hang a poster of the Big Three—
Bigfoot, the Loch Ness monster,
and the Abominable Snowman—
with the word *Believe*.

Lisa spreads out her books
and her journals.

We build beds
from foam rubber pads,
sleeping bags, old pillows.
Sleeping mats, we call them.

This is where we want to be.

Before Picture

The Diet Book
suggests I take a *before* picture.

It makes sense to me,
even if I hate photos of myself.

Lisa suggests we go down to the beach,
stand near the lifeguard,
with the beach in the background.
Pick suggests we hike up a small hill.
I choose the nursery,
just to get it over with.
I stand on the deck,
the sky blue like crystal,
and the air smells
like brine.
Last night, millions of anchovies
washed onto the shore.
The beach is thick with sand crabs.
The seagulls pitch and dive
from the mountains to the beach
like I've never seen before,
lunging into the sand,
out of control.

I feel every cell swirling around,
my metabolism churning
starving, fighting.

So, in some moment of foolishness
or bravery or maybe both,
I step onto the deck,
　　　　take off my shirt,
and hold it over my head.
My pale skin
absorbs the naked sun.
Pick and Lisa laugh,
but not at me, I think.
They are in the moment,

me with my shirt off,
swinging it around my head,
the chaos and screech of the seagulls.
My body shudders
in the sudden wonder
of a decision finally made.

What if I'm not alone?
What if Pick and Lisa
and maybe others might help me?
What if all this matters less than I think it does?

Let's do this! I cry out.
I pump my fist in the air
because I don't know what else to do.

Without asking,
Pick and Lisa step onto the deck with me,
stand next to me on either side.
My mother snaps the photo.
Let me see, Lisa yells, and she
gets the phone from my mom,
stares at it, and makes a funny face,
then she runs across the deck
while we chase her.

In the photo,
my friends are on either side,
Pick, his smart, handsome face beaming,
Lisa, her chin lowered, eyes wide,
born for the camera,
and me, so much wider
than both of them.

....

It's not fair, I think,
how my sides overflow my shorts,
or the way my legs
always rub together.

I'm not sure I can do this.

We print the photo
and pin it to a shelf
beneath two trolls,
one holding a tiny flowerpot,
the other a hatchet.

Then we go to the beach,
run the whole way
until our toes reach the shore,
lay our bodies down
in the warm sand.

At the nursery,
the seagulls land on the fence,
stuffed or tired.

Level 1 Induction

I miss apples
pizza
French toast
sandwiches
candy
watermelon

hamburger buns
cake
pizza
doughnuts
spaghetti
chips
pizza

It's been a week.

The Kid Who Draws at the Beach

At the beach
we meet this kid named Jorge.
He is often by himself,
building sandcastles
or sketching something
inside a brown journal.
He says he takes the bus a few miles
from Bolinas.
He likes *the feel* of traveling.

We like him right away.

Loch Ness Monster

Pick holds up a drawing
of a tentacled creature,
a giant, mutant squid
rising out of the bay.
Our game needs more enemies,

he says. *What do you think?*
The robots need
to face a real threat.

I reach for *Mysterious World*,
flip it open to chapter 6,
"Creatures of Lakes and Lochs,"
hold it up in the air
like I just found the answer
we've been looking for.

Something like this? I ask.
Pick nods. *Maybe?*
But isn't that the Loch Ness monster?
Yes! I say. *What if—*I turn the page—
in the game, Earth is filled
with these creatures,
but they aren't enemies.
They are just lost,
isolated, angry, afraid,
creatures that just don't
quite fit in?
What if part of the game
is to help these creatures
stop destroying things
and become allies?
Pick looks at me.
I'm not sure that makes it fun, Ari,
but you really like that one, don't you.

It's true. The Loch Ness
monster is one of my
favorite mysteries,

my first cryptozoological research
into something out there
beyond our explanation.

In fourth grade, we watched
a movie about *unexplained phenomena*
that showed in *never-been-seen-before* animation
four adorable, long-necked aquatic dinosaurs
swimming freely from the ocean
and up a long canal
inland to the mountains,
swimming, playing, living.

Gradually, as they make their way home,
the water changes, the earth shifts,
mountains turn into the sea.
Slowly the land closes,
until finally
it swallows itself
and forms the lake.

The dinosaurs are cut off
from their species.
Isolated, a few families
alone in a giant mountain lake.

In the cartoon,
their smiling faces turn upside down.

A graph of fish types
pops up on the screen,
and as the years roll by,

the colorful fish
disappear, one by one.

The ones left behind
thrive as best they can,
but the cool rain
mixes with the salt;
the brackish water,
becomes fresher and fresher.
Slowly the dinosaurs,
over a thousand generations,
turn from dinosaurs
      to lake monsters,
long and serpentine,
shorter teeth,
wider paddles,
out of space and time,
until finally,
this one tiny lake monster
is the only one left,
afraid
    of itself,
lost in a memory
      it can't understand.

It dives into
the loch,
eight hundred feet down
so it isn't seen,
its bulk too great,
the fish too small,
the pike, the char,

even the stickleback
runs thin.

It doesn't belong here,
bloated, outdated, long-necked
and long-toothed,
its tail swirling in the choppy waters.

After generations,
it knows that people
are staring at it,
gathering on the shoreline,
the edge of the castle,
near the forest,
to see its murky form
even as it tries
to skim trout near
the surface or see
the colors swirl
in the reflections of the sun
from underneath.

It misses the light,
swims the span of the lake
        looking for an opening
                between the worlds,

a memory inside
its DNA,
its soul,
something more
        that it's never seen
                but can't stop looking for.

Home,
other creatures like itself.
It needs to know that
it isn't some mistake.

In the cartoon,
the people on the boat
wear yellow raincoats,
throw a party for Nessie,
celebrate as the three
ancient humps arc out of the water,
    and then, in rainbow verse
across the screen
for the viewers,
What do you think?

The tail of the lake monster
coils around the words.

Pick walks over to me,
I look up from my memory,
the book clutched tightly in my hands.
He looks at the pages,
points to a glossy, fake-looking
photo of Nessie.
*We should definitely
have some monsters
in the game*, he says,
*and they should be
fighting for good.*

Ketosis

I am eating myself.
My body fights,
accumulates ketones,
fat breaking down,
starving for carbohydrates,
sugar, everything it can remember.
Everything it once knew,
washed away into waste.

My body remembers,
especially my tongue,
the way the crust of pizza
marries the cheese and sauce.

My body remembers
the juicy splendor
of an orange cut open,
the creaminess
of a banana,
an apple dipped in honey.

My body remembers
a night in the city
when my father
handed me a five,
sent me down the street
for Hostess cupcakes
and lemon fruit pies.

But my body also remembers
hands that push

and reach, back and forth,
because a kid my size *can take it.*

My body remembers
the tetherball court,
too many names, too many hands,
too many voices in the circle
around the game.

My body remembers
the crying rage,
throwing Jay to the ground,
fist after fist
and the solid knock
of knuckles and flesh
and blood and blond hair
and wiry braces.

My body remembers.

My body is fighting itself,
and in its desperation,
it's eating its fat.

There Is a Space

In the morning,
when I put on my shorts,
I feel something odd.
There is a space, no bigger than
the tip of my pinkie,
between the waistline of my shorts

and my body.
I put my finger inside the space
and walk outside
beneath the grape arbor.
I whisper to myself,
in a sacred tone,
It's working.
I check all day
to see if the space is still there.

How Many Pounds?

The scale
lives in the kitchen,
so on Fridays
I step onto it
and write down on a sticky note
the number it says.

After one week,
the number is lower by two.

Studio Days

Every day with Pick and Lisa,
we make art,
shoot bows and arrows,
do chores.
We carry moist clay bricks,
twenty-five pounds each,
into stacks at the back

of the gallery, place them
where the Artist needs them.

One brick a week for us.
We work on our trolls,
fill shelves
and empty spaces
with mischievous creatures.
At lunch, I eat burgers with no buns,
and salad, bring cheese-and-meat roll-ups wherever I go.
Pick and Lisa try to eat like I do.
I tell them they don't have to,
and sometimes they share bags of chips
or candy, but they try their best
not to do it around me,
and I am starting to feel stronger.
Each week, I weigh myself.
I slowly watch the numbers change.

At night we watch the stars swirl
through the skylight,
listen to the sounds of people
walking around town.
Sometimes we open the studio
and have art shows.

We talk about our dreams,
pretend they are windows into the future.
We gather at the breakfast table,
a circle of prophets.
Lisa talks about a dream
where I'm wearing a white-and-green
Hawaiian shirt, and I'm skateboarding

in a school parking lot.
In the dream, she says, I am half of myself.
I smile, try to imagine it,
and for the first time,
it feels possible,
but I wonder
what it would mean
if I actually lose half
of who I am?

Shore Break

We go to the beach.
Lisa teaches us that
at least once a day
you have to put your feet
in the ocean. We lie in the sand
without towels.
We learn to bodysurf,
pulling our heads up and out
just before we slam down
on the churning sand.

Jorge

Bolinas Ridge,
I tell Lisa. *We need to do it*.
She smiles, lets the sand
filter through her fingers.
Lisa's eyes squint
at the sun above me.

I feel the sand shift behind,
off-balance.
Jorge towers there.
His skin and hair are dark.
His words are swallowed
in his smile.
I heard you say Bolinas Ridge?
I hike there all the time.

He talks about
living here his whole life.
We ask him lagoon questions
and about the hippies
who live in Bolinas.
He tells us they like
to remove the highway
signs to keep people away.

Sometimes My Father Comes

Some days
my father drives out to see us,
but he won't stay.
Sometimes he takes
a drive with my mother.
Sometimes, after the drive,
they stand at the car
just outside the gate.
Their voices are drums
booming without any measure.
We watch through the gate
until the giant form of my father

turns to come in and say good-bye.
He makes promises.
We'll go to the comic store,
we'll take a hike near Inverness,
I'll show you the elk
on the peninsula.
He hugs me.

My mother stands near the dirt and gravel
where the Sunbird was parked.
She won't come in for a long time.

Shopping

One morning,

we go to the outlet stores.
I refuse to go in.

Mom takes Lisa inside.
I sit in the car,
the air thickening,
the heat pushing down
on the leather seats,
reading *Ogre, Ogre*
by Piers Anthony.
Smash the half ogre
is trying to solve
a vague dissatisfaction
about himself,
some discomfort
lodged in his mind

and body,
like the slow tick
of a faraway clock.
He decides
at last
to seek help.

Hours (maybe) later,
Lisa and my mother
come out of the store,
bending and swaying
like apple trees,
overloaded branches
with translucent plastic bags
of clothes and shoes.

Lisa smiles at me.

When we reach the nursery,
they have a fashion show
in the courtyard.
Clothes pile up on the wooden floor
and in front of the huge mirror,
where Lisa spins in skirts,
some tight, some overflowing.
Tight-fitting T-shirts, rifting at the belly,
and flowering blouses,
the sculptures looking on
in tranquil indifference.

I see her joy,
and I feel my fire.
I've always liked the way she looks,

but when I see her so happy
in her colorful new clothes,
it feels as if a hand is reaching
through my stomach
and into my chest,
pulling at my heart
until I can't breathe.

I want to tell her something
about how she looks,
but I don't.

Lisa sings some song into the mirror,
lifting her hair out of the collar
of her new pink shirt.
She turns to her side,
poses with her chin lowered,
her blond hair
falling slightly over her eyes.
How do I look? she asks.
My body is burning.
I walk over to where she is,
and I stand near the mirror.

Smile.

This place, I think, was made for her.

Lisa looks toward the gate.
She looks back to me,
and her steady hands
land on my shoulders.

....

Thank you, she whispers.
For what? I ask, smiling.
But she doesn't answer.

Maps

Pick comes later that day with his mom.
She wants to see the nursery.
We spend the afternoon
outside with a bucket of markers,
pastels, and old paints,
drawing maps for the game.
Pick loves to draw maps,
and Lisa draws in the borders.
Sometime in the afternoon,
we decide to make a map
of the gallery so we can
always remember.

See You July Fourth

That evening
Pick goes
home with his mom.
He has to start some kind of camp
in Sausalito for one week.
I promise to work on the game.
I'll be back for the Fourth of July!
he says. *Try to think
about the damage charts.*
I promise I will.

I try, but I don't think about them at all.
    Not once.

The Walk

Lisa carries a backpack
that unfolds into a beach chair.
The effortless straps
curl around her shoulders,
push her chest out.
Her white shark-tooth necklace
falls down the center.
Her blond hair,
in a wavy drop
to the middle of her back,
pushes around
her blue bikini,
rainbow sandals
edging perfectly along
the beach path.

I am just behind her,
too slow
for her determined walk,
her mirrored aviator sunglasses,
her pursed lips,
her focus.

By the beach path,
some older boys
get between us,

walk next to her.
They talk to her,
but she hides behind
her mirrored glasses.

It's not just how slow I am.
It's that I'm afraid.
I shrink back
in these moments
and realize how young I am.
I mean, I sculpt trolls
out of clay
and design role-playing games
with my best friend.
I'm on a diet
where I can't even eat bread.

These boys
with football hands
and chalky blond hair,
strange smells
and too many muscles.
What can *I* do?

Lisa stops in the sand
and looks back at me.
Her body turns sideways,
and she holds out her hand
for mine.

Elysium at the Beach

We find our spot
almost all the way to the water.
She spreads out her chair
and breathes.
Slowly she unpacks
her things,
water, lotion, books.
She's reading two now,
A Wrinkle in Time
and a romance novel.

Lisa rubs sunscreen
on her legs.
I stare at the water
as much as I can,
until she asks,
Get my back?
My hands shake.
I tell myself,
like a brother,
like a friend,
just a friend,
but it doesn't matter.
Her skin feels smooth
in my hands.
I let myself do it slowly,
a little embarrassed.
She trusts me to do this.
She is aware of every moment.
She's not afraid of what I'm feeling.
It doesn't change how she treats me.

Later, after we swim,
we talk about characters
from the stories we write.
Elysium, she-warrior,
driven out of her
village as a young girl,
captured, made a servant,
learned to fight
in the gladiator pits,
until one day,
with the help of Thall,
she escaped.

Jorge's House

Later that week
Jorge invites us to dinner,
even my mother.
It's just him and his mom,
in a one-bedroom house
near the Bolinas school,
through redwood groves.

His house is
filled with cooking pots
and yellow plates
on the red walls.
Over the fireplace,
black-and-white photos
of men on horseback,
and a well-dressed couple

from long ago.
On a long wooden table,
his mom
is placing
silver plates
with different foods
in circle patterns,
yellow cheese,
a pile of almonds,
some cold fish like the herring
my father eats,
some meat on skewers.
There are several plates
of purple, black, and green olives.

My mother walks
right to her,
places her hand on the fabric
of her long blue skirt,
and starts in
on the beauty
of the fabric,
the smell of the food.
Jorge tells us to have some
sopes. Lisa does.
I eye the bread and almonds,
but I stay with ham and slabs of
     cheese.

At dinner,
Lisa pours some wine in her cup
when no one is looking.

. . . .

Jorge helps to translate
when his mother speaks too fast
and her words roll from English
to Spanish and back again.

For dessert,
his mother holds a plate
with two hands,
sets it on the center of the table.
Brazo de reina,
she mouths out loud,
a rolled-up cake
filled with cream
surrounded by fruit
that look like hand grenades.
Cherimoya, Jorge says.
Ice cream fruit.
And it is,
like ice cream on my tongue.
I take a bite of the cake,
one flaky, delicious bite,
taste the sugar and vanilla cream.
For a moment, I want to eat it all,
but then Jorge's mother
tells a joke about Jorge
being the tallest boy since first grade,
and Lisa can't stop laughing,
and then I can't stop laughing,
and I put down my fork.
I feel good.
One bite
is just
enough.

Saint George

After dinner
the grown-ups drink
thick-smelling coffee,
and we linger near the door,
eager to go out
under the stars.
Wait, wait, wait,
his mother calls,
pulls us in
to the couches
to tell us the story
of how Jorge
is actually
Saint George.

Jorge covers his eyes
with long, dark-brown fingers.
He doesn't want to hear the story.

At his church,
when he was nine,
at a prayer meeting
in the glow of the stained glass
Jorge placed his hand
on the purple shoulder
of a man bent over in pain,
a heart attack, or
a broken heart.
He offered a prayer,
spoke in a voice,
they say,

that was not his own,
and when it was over,
the man stood up
in perfect health,
his knees soaked
in tears and sweat.
They say that
Jorge's was the voice
of the Holy Ghost.
They say that the room,
from the altar to the door,
grew wild with
yellow and green
light, and flecks of gold dust
filled the air.

Lisa looks at me.
Real gold? I ask.
Jorge smiles shyly,
shrugs like he can't believe
it happened either.
Shhh, my mother
tells us to quiet down,
sips her coffee.

They say
that day that Jorge's
legs grew longer.
That's why he's so tall.

Jorge presses his legs close
together like he's
trying to hide them.

When word got out,
the church fathers
met over seven Sundays,
and finally they
made him a local saint.

We look at my mother.
She shifts in her seat.
Beautiful story, she says,
her face warm,
her body relaxed.
Like the midrash
your grandpa tells.
I love it.

When the story ends,
we walk outside and look toward
the forests on the hills,
make plans to hike Bolinas Ridge
before the summer ends.

10 Pounds

By the end of June
I've lost 10 pounds.

A bag of rice,
a bowling ball,
a cat,
three big bottles
of soda.

My shorts are looser,
and I can fit two whole fingers
between the waistline
and my body.

At lunch,
my mother hands me a bag
of veggie "pork" rinds,
sour cream and onion.
I eat them all.

Lisa and I
sit in our part of the gallery
sculpting trolls.
We try to teach Jorge
how to do it,
our hands coated in clay.
By now they have
driftwood bases,
shells and dried sticks,
rocks and bark.

Even when I sit,
my shirt feels loose.
        Loose.
Something, for once, fits.

Mitzvot

My mother puts her hand on my shoulder,
reminds me

that pretty soon
I will need to
think about meeting
with the rabbi again.
My bar mitzvah is in the fall;
I'm already so late.
I need to prepare:

       a.   Ask Questions
       b.   Study Hebrew
       c.   Do Mitzvot

I remember, just before we moved,
my grandma's Brooklyn
apartment, the smell
of oily latkes and candle wax.
It's late, and I am sitting on
my father's knee,
stacking four quarters,
knocking them down,
stacking them again.
They talked like grown-ups,
the low hum of my grandfather's
voice, each word half-full
of breath and accent.
They started to argue about
my bar mitzvah,
where it will be,
when it will happen,
and I felt my father
shift in his chair until
I finally slid down

and sat on the floor
beneath the table.

Grandma reached beneath,
took my hand,
and led me to the kitchen.
Why don't you sit down?
I'll make you some oatmeal.
I ate it, played with tiny
sword letter openers.
I could hear
the voices
rise and fall
and mix together,
angry or frustrated,
a pot boiling over
and simmering again.

I ate the oatmeal.
Ari, she said, smiling with hope,
how will you keep the mitzvot?
When I didn't know what she meant,
she told me that the mitzvot
are our commandments,
the good deeds we do
and how we behave,
honoring our parents,
helping others,
observing the Sabbath.

I remember a time
when we walked

to the grocery store
and a man with a torn
jacket, his beard long
and gray, asked my grandma
for some food. I hid
behind her while
she handed him
a five-dollar bill,
and the loaf of challah
we had just bought.
The man said nothing
and walked away.
She stood, watching him go,
then turned to me and whispered,
You see, mitzvot. We do because we do.

My Father Comes

When we get back from the beach,
my father is there.
Finally, he says,
sits up, his black hair
curled in different directions.
Come 'ere, kid.
I feel small next to him.
He listens as I tell him about 10 pounds.
He smiles, makes it the biggest
news in the world.
I'm proud of you, he says.
You look great.

....

I ask him if he's staying over.
Just tonight, he says.

At bedtime,
I read and listen to
the familiar beat of their voices,
arguments in undulating rhythms
of light and dark,
his deep voice
rolling out
in a wave of
reason, smooth
and weighted.

When they get quiet,
I walk to get some water.
He's holding some papers,
a stack of letters or something.
Across the table,
her eyes look out the window.
It's a silence I don't understand.

I pour a glass of water,
but they don't notice.

On the top of the fridge
is a red bag, shiny and full
like a Mylar balloon.
I saw it when I first came in.
    Doritos.
Of course, he must have brought them,
and why would he think about

my diet?
I wait silently in the kitchen
until their voices start again.
I reach for the bag.
I feel a rush in my body,
and in a moment
I'm back in my room.

I sit on the edge of my mat.
The dim light of my reading lamp
illuminates the red foil,
the wedged chip,
a perfect triangle
of texture and salt.
The bag sits between
my legs, and I notice
how the fat on my legs doesn't seep
out of my shorts as much,
that my stomach feels small
in my pajamas.
For a moment, I imagine
that the chips in this bag
will bring it all back.
I imagine that maybe
I deserve it all back.

I look into the bag.

I think of Pick
asking me who I am,
look over at Lisa sleeping.
I think of my before picture
and how far I've come.

I feel the sand in my toes,
and the warm sun
and ocean air.
I'm desperate.
I want to hold my diet book
like holy scripture,
to pray a spell of protection
over my soul,
but I don't.

Instead,
I open the bag,
feel the salt of the first chip
settle on my tongue.
The taste blocks the noise.

I don't stop
until the sides
have all been licked clean.

July

— Promises

The Diet Book promises that Four Beautiful Things will
  happen:

1. I will be free from hunger.
    I still want ice cream all the time.

2. I will notice an increase in well-being.
    I do feel better.

3. I will notice the pounds dropping off.
    *Let them drop into the abyss. Let them
    scream as they fall.*

4. I will experience a decrease in measurements
    that the tape measure can tell me about in detail.
    Will I still need to go to the big and tall shop?

Then He Left

When I get out of the shower,
I hear the sliding metal
of my father's keys.
I dry off,
get dressed,
and walk out to see him.
Ari, he says.
Sit down.
His words
are thick paste.
He says he has to go away,
get some money for the business.
Things are tough.
I'll be back soon, Ari,
but I have to go away for a while.
Don't worry, he says. *I have a plan.*
I smile. Look at his eyes. Take a deep breath.
I believe him. He lifts his duffel bag by the door,
the keys to the Sunbird
already in his
hand.
  He leans over,
        kisses me on the forehead.
I love you, you mensch,

                         and he goes.

July Fourth

I

Pick's mom drops him off in the morning.
We spend the day at the beach,
and by sunset we sit on the roof.
Me, Pick, Lisa
position ourselves
for the fireworks.
The roof feels safe
and far away from everything.
We watch the cars
in a radiant line
from the mountain road
shining into every beach lot.
Families shift street to street,
streamers, flags, sparklers,
the occasional POP.

We eat sunflower seeds,
spit the shells into the dirt
far below us.

Pick spits a seed into the distance,
looks straight ahead.
I have to go to Australia, he says.
What! I say. *Why?*
It's a family reunion, mate.
He fakes an accent.

I feel the summer suddenly shrink.

....

How come you didn't tell me? I ask.
We have plans.
He holds out his hands,
folds them into fists.
Because I didn't want you to get mad.

I understand what he means.
I don't like change.

II
The fireworks
bloom above the cobalt sea.
Pick and Lisa talk about Australia.

Later, at the nursery,
we look over the game,
our pencils scratch paper.
We draw a new class of robots
that can shift their shapes,
adapt to their environment.
Lisa is taking pictures
when Pick mumbles,

I'm sorry I'm so mean to you.
He looks away.

That day, when we were packing,
when you said you didn't
tell your parents about the bike path?
I got mad because I thought
we would have to hide it forever,
or that you just didn't trust me enough
because I ran away.

I wanted you to change
so you could stop being so bad to yourself,
but I'm the one who was afraid.

Pick doesn't look up when he says this.
His eyes focus on a quadrant
of the paper where he draws
a giant metallic foot.
I am quiet too.

     I just hated it. I hated them.

Pick's voice trails back
into the past.
He's remembering,
but the experience
is lightning
striking now.
He doesn't wipe his tears,
lets each one spill into his mouth
until they swirl with his words.

With his pencil,
he scratches a crude line
along the center of the boxed page.

We were riding. Just riding.
                  What happened? Lisa asks.
I forget that she doesn't know.
He traces the pencil along the line
on the paper. He draws a circle
around Dolan Avenue and an arrow
to the Mill Valley/Sausalito bike path.

His mind overflowing onto the paper,
he talks in pencil
scratches and shaded images.
I concentrate on his drawings,
see it all in my mind.
He draws an *X* halfway
to Sycamore Avenue and stops.

I should have done more,
but I just kept riding.
I let you down.

I look at him over the table.
I think of jokes
but don't say them.
His body shakes,
like he might break in half.

It's okay, I say.
He shifts in his chair, grabs his pencil tight.
He draws stick figures near the *X*.

It's not, he says through gritted teeth.
It's
          not okay.
                    You . . . Suddenly fierce,
he points the pencil at me, eraser first.
He gets up, one hand in a fist.
I stand up too.

          You
          should
          have

done
more . . .
You

    just SAT THERE,
while they did those things to you.

HOW COULD YOU LET THEM?

            how could I let them??

I get up, walk over to him.
In my mind is the rhythm of some speech
I will never give.
I stare straight at him
with sudden courage.

I don't know why, I say.
I don't know why I didn't fight back.
Maybe I should have. But I couldn't.
I don't want to fight that way.

Face flushed,
Pick looks at me,
red with anger and tears.
Suddenly he grabs my shoulders
with both hands,
vibrates an inhuman growl,

Why didn't
        I
            do anything?
                . . . .

His breath lingers at *I*.
He's desperate for an answer
I can't give him.

I'm a coward! he shouts,
lets go of my shoulders,
his face steaming with guilt and rage.
He rips the graph paper,
tries to break the pencil,
but it's too small. He throws it instead.

I want to think of a joke,
or something wise
about how we are all afraid,
or some obscure fact about a chupacabra,
about the game or the beach.
I look at Lisa, but she's quietly drawing.

He walks around the room,
then finally just sits,
his arms folded over his knees.
He mutters,

I was mad at myself.
                    I took it out on you.

I walk over,
sit down next to him,
pull out two fresh sheets
of graph paper,
and slowly I start
filling in squares
until he starts to do it too.

Bigfoot Versus Yeti

Later that night,
on my sleeping mat,

I stare at the darkened shapes
in the old wooden room,
and it hits me, the *why* of it.
A clear thought like starlight,
the kind that only comes
after something tough happens.
I click on the flashlight,
dig around for a marker,
pull an old picture off the wall,
and start to sketch.

I draw a bad picture of Bigfoot:
brown fur, giant feet,
long arms and longer teeth.
Pick, wake up and look at this picture.
He makes a noise, and I go again.
Bigfoot or yeti, Pick? Look.
And it's like this for a while,
me holding up my Bigfoot picture,
asking him to decide if it's
Bigfoot or a yeti.

Pick whispers, in a sleepy
yawn, *That's Bigfoot?*
I laugh. *What if I tell you
it's a yeti?*
What? Pick says.
It's a yeti, I say.

It's Bigfoot, he says.
Look at the brown fur.
Everyone knows yetis have white fur.
It's a yeti, I say. *A yeti. Yeti.*
Yeti. Maybe it's a southern yeti.
Maybe it's the summer. Yeti all the way.
How can you know? You don't.
Fine! he yells, defeated. *Yeti.*
>   *NO!* I shout.
>   *It's Bigfoot!*
He looks confused,
sleepy in the dull light.
Do you get it? I say.
Everyone thinks the yeti
and Bigfoot are the same,
but they are completely
different creatures!

If you call something a name enough times,
maybe you just accept it.

Everyone knows that the yeti
is found in Arctic climates, the Himalayas.
He's the Abominable Snowman.
Bigfoot is a Sasquatch, native to North America!
Everyone knows that they are different creatures,
but they just make them the same
because they don't even TRY
to look at who they REALLY are.

Fine, he grumbles, *fine. Can I sleep now?*
and drops down to his pillow.

....

I let people call me names
because that's what
they've always done.
I let them make me into who I am.

Some of the biggest lies I ever told
were the ones I told myself.

I'm too fat
I'm not good enough
They will never like me

I don't have to accept that everyone
else says that Bigfoot is a yeti,
when I know the truth.
Each animal is its own self.

There's a possibility of a different
truth. Maybe I *can* be someone different
when I wake up.
Not Bigfoot *or* a yeti.
Maybe it isn't even that I want to only lose
        weight.

Maybe I want to find the real me.

Pick

We drop Pick off at the Dolan house,
say hello and good-bye
to his parents.

....

He gives me
his manila folder,
his graph paper,
an envelope full
of drawings.
Take these, he says.
Work on Alcatraz Base while I'm gone.
It's the starting point for the players.
Make it solid.
I promise I will.
Later, Pick! I tell him.
Have fun flying
a million hours
to Australia.
Watch out for the bunyips!

People always leave.

At the bottom of the stairs,
one of the slats on the railing
is slightly broken, so it snaps
if you touch it as you walk by.
This time
down the stairs,
I break
the whole piece
right off.

She Doesn't See It

I don't see it, you know?
At the breakfast table,

I'm eating eggs and cheese.
Lisa is eating toast.
She tries to eat what I eat,
but she tells me that sometimes
a body just wants some toast.

In my silence,
she gives me more words,
quiet little gifts
that hit the right places.
No, I'm serious, I don't get it, she says,
the whole fat thing.
I mean, I understand
how you might feel bad
when other kids are idiots,
but why do you let it bother you?

She pauses.
I look down at my eggs.

So what if there's more of you?

I love all her words.
They have so much power.
She is listening,
paying attention,
like a friend should.
She doesn't cancel how I feel,
dismiss it
or wrap it up
in a different way.
She lets my pain be real to her too,
but she also makes

me feel strong, like what others
say doesn't matter at all.

Lisa spreads gobs of butter on her toast,
lifts the knife, and smiles.
No carbs, right?
We laugh.
I stare at the toast
for a long, long time.
I imagine the crunch
of bread in my teeth.
How can someone
never have bread again?
This can't go on forever.

Long, Good Days

Days stretch,
yawning dogs
with straightening backs.

We swim under the sun.
We don't care who we are.

Today is every day
and tomorrow.

If I could stop time here,
I would pull the cold
handle of the moon
to my face,
order it to

shift its weight
and make
everything
a steady ocean.

Baby Huey

We walk back from the beach,
the sunset behind us.
Lisa and I are laughing.
Jorge hums,
carries his boogie board
on top of his head.

Ahead of us at the crosswalk
of the last parking lot,
beneath a tall redwood,
two older boys are drinking
out of coffee mugs.
Bare-chested, shirts
tied around their waists,
they laugh loudly
when they see us.
They stare at Lisa,
her shoulders back, blond hair
falling over her blue bikini.

Beautiful.

She has told me over and over
that it doesn't matter.
Silly boys, she always says. *Just all silly boys.*

I hope they don't say anything,
but the air is too heavy
for silence,
and the words
creep out
between
the sounds
of the cars driving by.

What's up, Baby Huey?

They are looking at Lisa,
but they are talking
        to me.

Way to go, Baby Huey. They nod, laugh,
and the blond one comes behind me.
I try to ignore him,
but he's too close.
When I turn,
he is imitating
my side-to-side walk.

Why don't you guys leave us alone!
Lisa says without even looking.

Baby Huey's got a girrrrrlfriend.

How can it be
that just a few seconds ago
everything was perfect?

Jorge asks them to stop.
They call him a beanpole.

When we get to a stop sign,
the cars are climbing away from
    Stinson,
a long line east on Shoreline Highway.

What did it look like
to the family in the white Suburban
or to that older couple
in the red convertible?
We're just
grains of sand,
stepped on
or wiped off,
washed away.

I tell myself the familiar
things:
Ride it out. Ignore them.
Let the voices fade.
They're not going to hurt you.
    But I remember the bike path,
    feel the bruises all over my body.

The boys keep walking
next to us until finally
Lisa stomps her feet.
Her voice is shrill.
    You are so unoriginal. Just go away!

They step back.
The dark-haired boy
looks down,
puts his face in his shirt,
takes a long breath,
then looks at his friend.
> *Come on, man.*
He waves his shirt
toward the road
in a gesture of retreat
or surrender.
He looks at Lisa,
whispers something.

Cars idle in the dusk.
The tide is coming in.
C'mon, leave the kids alone,
the dark-haired one says.
The blond one laughs.
Later, Baby Huey.

Later, a-holes! Lisa shouts.

Jorge hoists the boogie board
back to the top of his head.
I walk as straight as I can.

Later, on the sleeping mats,
I slam my face into my pillow.
I keep seeing it all in my head.
Not just today. All the days.
I try to put everything into the pillow,

crying, laughing, like I'm going crazy.
Lisa walks over to me and kneels down,
puts her hand on my back.
Don't listen to them.
Don't listen.

Robots

In the morning,
I'm still thinking
about the walk back
from the beach.
I decide to work on the game
to get my mind off things.
I take out graph paper
from our *game-creation supplies.*
I squint my eyes
at the paper,
tiny boxes edged together,
turn them invisible,
sketch robots
to scale.

First I draw a car:
four boxes long,
two boxes high.

A truck:
six boxes long
three boxes high.

. . . .

And then the guardian robot,
five boxes,
its muscular metal leg
the fortified steel frame,
the housing for the pilot,
the cockpit in the helmet,
all rise twenty boxes high.

One metallic arm
reaches out
nine boxes toward the square sun (four boxes).

In the distance,
    the guardian robots
    watch over the bridge,
    steel plates
    against their
    nuclear hearts.

cO-lec-tOrs

The next day, back at the beach,
the water is perfect,
and we don't see those boys again.
Sun-beaten and saltwater-bleached,
we return to the nursery before the sun sets.

A man in a silver shirt
shines near a woman in light blue.
They wear sunglasses inside,
lean on the counter,
turning pages

of print portfolios,
talking low.

Lisa turns to me. *Who are they?*
I nod and whisper,
with a long *o* sound,
cO-lec-tOrs.
Lisa nods, smiles a little.
Well, she says, pursing her lips.
I seeee.

My mother
glides in
holding a pink bottle,
champagne and glasses.

She talks as she pours.
The foam bubbles up and over,
and she wipes the counter
in one stylish movement.
She believes that champagne
is the drink of a queen,
sophisticated, transformative.

We sit in the courtyard near *Melinda*,
watch the feral beach cats walk
the top of the fence.

The collectors ask questions.
The Artist answers,
disjointed and familiar phrases,
names of sculptures:
The Ice Priest *is a reincarnation of the Mother Spirit.*

The Lotus Keeper *is the guardian of the sacred flower.*
There is an opening in the head of the creature
for the life force to come and go as it pleases.

More champagne.

She clears her throat, signals us
to get salami and crackers.
In the back, we pull Ritz from boxes
and arrange them in a semicircle
on a floral platter.
We build a cheese tower,
place salami in a red sea around it.
I fold cheese squares and salami into my mouth
with my left hand. With my right,
I hold a cracker to my nose.
I can feel the golden flakiness and crunch
on my tongue.

The woman smiles.
We are interested in the entire collection.
My mother shakes her head in disbelief.
This is what she's been waiting for.
They talk for a long time.

Later,
the Artist walks them to the gate.
She smiles, closes it behind them.
The sun is down now.

Did they buy it? I ask.
No, Ari, they did not. She sighs.
But they might? She puts her

hands on my head.
I'm taller than her now,
but I still fit in her hands.
It's not that simple, Ari.
She breathes in and exhales words with no air.
Your father should be here.
He does the business. Closes the deals.

Her body moves past me.
I try to think of excuses for him,
but there aren't any.

Headlights of cars
filter through the gate.
I watch the soulless
face of the *Lotus Keeper*.
His eyes are closed,
his cracked terra-cotta hands
domed over
his perfect clay flower.

She's right.
He should
be here.

Two Champagne Bottles

Half-full,
pink and bubbling,
cheese tower, salami,
rising under the moon,
the Artist asleep in the back room.

The gate to the outside world is locked.
Lisa takes my hand.

Champagne, on average,
holds between three and twenty grams of
    carbohydrates.
But I am not thinking about *The Diet Book*.
I am thinking about Lisa,
still in her navy-blue bikini, white
button-down shirt over her shoulders.

We are sprites in the dark kitchen.
I hold a glass near my nose,
watch bubbles squeeze, pop,
  and explode into my nostrils.

I stare at the pinkish liquid.
Lisa stands on the other side of the counter.
Cheers, she says,
holds her glass toward me in the air.
She is giving me something that is just for us.
She smiles. Her lips form around the edge.

Drinks are not new for her.
Once, the doctors told Lisa she should never drink,
that she might get sick like her mother.

I drink.
It burns.
I cough.
The bubbles jam my throat.
I hold it down until it turns
into pops of laughter,

our hands over our mouths,
champagne on the counter,
on the floor. I feel my fingertips,
like they are separate from my body.
We try to stay quiet, pour glass after glass.
Lisa can drink it so fast. I take one sip at a time.
We laugh until we knock the salami and cheese
to the floor. We scramble to the far side
of the counter. Did we wake her?

I hold my breath, but trying not to laugh
makes it harder. We huddle close,
her hands on my shoulders,
now my knees,
her blond hair
in my hair now,
    and she looks me in my eyes.
The fire, the champagne, the fear makes me numb
until I feel her grip, close above my knee,
and I squirm, tickled into uselessness,
    but she doesn't stop.
Her hands are on my body.
I feel her fingers climb beneath my shirt,
reach over my love handles, onto my stomach.

No one has ever touched my stomach.

For a moment, I feel shame like cold water,
and I turn on my side. She doesn't stop,
but I'm okay.

She laughs louder.
I reach for her hand,

feel the length of her shoulder, her arm.
That's it, I say, laughing.
Don't make me sit on you.
Her hands finally tired,
she surrenders
in quiet laughter,
      breath,
         cheese,
               the unexpected warmth
                       of bodies close

    beneath the countless stars.

After Champagne

Eyes open,
my head glued to the pillow,
my body pressed against the planked floor,
lost in wood and paint,
I feel my hair with tired hands
and find my heartbeat in the center
of my skull.
There is   no   other   sound.
I taste all of last night.

Lisa sits cross-legged
on the bench outside,
her hair a circlet
of gold straw.
She stares
into her phone.

           ....

My mother in the far corner
of the garden, coffee
steaming into the sky.

I am hungry.
I want a bagel with lox and cream cheese.
I want pancakes, French toast.
I want to dip my oranges in a pool of syrup.
I want bacon and eggs and a huge
plate of hash browns.

I slip *Mysterious World*
under my arm,
walk through the garden
in my socks, each step, dust,
each breath a question.
I want to ask Lisa
about the night before,
but when I sit down,
I'm too nervous,
and the questions all float away,
so instead I find other words.

You know, people always think
yeti and Bigfoot are the same.

But for once, I don't really
want to talk about this.
I wish I could find
the right words to say.

Closing the Gallery

Coffee-soaked
and exhausted,
my mother walks over to us.
She looks at my eyes.
I need you to stay with Lisa tonight
at her house.

She smiles at Lisa.
Your mom is back.
But I see she's nervous.
She doesn't like
leaving us at Lisa's house.
She unfolds sections
of her plans like a map,
points to ideas,
unexplored reasons:
busy meetings,
business dealings, unexpected
turns of events.
She calls it adventure,
like she's trying to be brave
for all the business she has to do.

Last night fades into
in-between places.

We pack our stuff for the drive
back to the world.

Lisa is in the back seat,
not feeling good.

. . . .

I want to tell her
how much fun
I had the night before.
I want to talk
about how much closer
I feel to her now,
how glad I am that she's my friend.
I want to ask
if she will float with me
over the Pacific
in champagne bubbles,
but she's curled up into
a morning glory,
petals folded
over her head,
silent as we wind our way
down Throckmorton Avenue.

Lisa's House

My mother coughs and smiles.
Okay, she says, *I should be back*
FIRST thing in the morning.
She reminds me to be polite,
to call if I need anything.
She hands me six five-dollar bills.
She makes me say her number out loud to her.
At times like this, she says,
I wish you did have your own phone.

I shrug.

. . . .

The long stairs to Lisa's house
wind in mossy disarray,
slate and stepping-stones
threaded through a leafy garden
between three old redwoods.
Swings creak on ancient branches,
and flowers reach into spots of sunlight.

Lisa's mom steps out from the front door.
She hugs my mom and me
and then her daughter.
Her body is strong,
her hair soaked
from a shower.
She smells like medicine
and daisies.

Ari! she says, and she runs her hand
over my body like I am a statue.
She puts her hand on my stomach
and under my chin.
You look so goood!
Her *o*'s roll the long way.
I try not to shrink back,
to feel and believe the words.

Her face wants to be beautiful,
like she is from some other world.
Her hands, long and thin,
spiraled in rings and bracelets
of gold and silver, shine.
Lisa takes my hand,
and we go inside.

The house is white,
filled with colorful pillows,
magazines, the smell of smoke.

We sit and play with her dogs,
twin Maltese with knotted fur.
She tries to hug them, but they
just keep jumping in and out of Lisa's lap.

Outside, the mothers
talk. Hands flail
in all directions,
stories and pronouncements,
bodies shifting.
It's normal for a moment,
and then I see my mom
grab Lisa's mom by the hands
with a painter's grip,
and she says something
eye to eye.

When they come in,
my mother kisses us both
and walks through the door.
Lisa's mom smiles
at us, walks to the kitchen,
pours a glass of wine,
and I feel the taste
of champagne
coming up from my stomach.
Lisa looks at her mom.
I see her shoulders suddenly
hunch forward, and

she takes my hand,
squeezes tightly,
her mouth forming
words she'll never say.

Fight the Corn Chip

Her mom gives me
a tuna fish sandwich,
rye bread, toasted, sliced in half,
corn chips stacked on the plate,
a Coke.

I already know that I'm not drinking
the soda, but I put a corn chip in my mouth.
I feel Lisa looking at me,
clear, green eyes, telling the story
of the boy who couldn't
fight the corn chip.
I take the edge of the chip,
scrape the tuna off the bread.
I place eight chips along the edge
of the tuna,
stack and eat them,
just the eight,
one by one.
The best chips I've ever had.

We spend the day on her phone.
I hate talking on the phone.
I don't know what to say,
but that's what we do.

We call her friend in Corte Madera,
a girl I've never met.
Lisa says a few words about me,
cute, shy, supercool,
hands me the phone and says,
Talk to Gretchen. She's totally funny.

Silence.

Lisa hits me in the leg, and grits her teeth. *Go!*

I say   hello.

Gretchen

Her phone voice is smooth, with a slight upward tilt
at the end of each sentence. It's scratchy too, in places.
She tells me that she has red hair. So red, she says,
it's orange. *It's, like, super rad,* she says.

She tells me that she likes vintage music,
just like we do.
Do you like glam rock bands
from the eighties? she says.
She tells me about Quiet Riot,
and how the names of the songs
are spelled in ways we shouldn't know about.
She sings to me, and she somehow gets me singing.

Come on feel the noise!
Girls, rock your boys!

. . . .

She stops in the middle,
makes sure that I am headbanging.
Lisa, in and out of the room,
doodling pastels on giant paper,
laughs and headbangs with me.

Later, Gretchen tells me I have a cute voice,
that we should get along,
no matter what we look like.

Glow-in-the-Dark Stars

Beneath glow-in-the-dark stars
we listen to Duran Duran.
I stare at Lisa's shelves:
a stuffed cat
with some of the whiskers
pulled out,
blue-and yellow-
painted frames filled
with old photographs
of people I don't know.
My favorite is one
of Lisa when
she was little,
standing on a dock
over a green pond,
fishing with her dad, I think.

On the dresser
is a jewelry box
swirled with necklaces

and plastic bracelets,
trinkets spread over
the top onto the floor.
One side of her room
is a picture window
covered in a rain forest curtain.
I stare at the eyeball of a tapir
peering out from
the mudbank.

I put my sleeping bag down.
Is your mom really gonna
let me sleep in here? I ask.
Yeah, Lisa says, *she doesn't care.*
We all sleep
in the planting room together,
don't we? Besides—she smiles—
I want you to see the stars.

Finally, near her door,
a vintage three-section concert poster
of Joe Elliott, the lead singer of Def Leppard,
in leather pants
and a Union Jack tank top.
In one frame,
he is leaning into the crowd.
In another he is standing,
playing air guitar with the band,
and, in the lower half, his face,
cradling the mic.
He isn't skinny in the poster,
but the crowd is still reaching
for him. He looks fierce. Unstoppable.

We spread out pencils and markers,
draw pictures.

She draws more pictures of Elysium,
the warrior queen, standing in the sun
on some high cliff.
Lisa is learning about perspective,
so she draws legs almost three-dimensionally,
stepping over a rise of green grass.

I draw my warrior, Thall, a hunter,
standing in the snow, his muscled arms
leaning on his spear
carved from a dragon's tooth.
He looks out toward the valley beyond.
He is waiting for something.
I want him to be a true hero,
imagine how he might be a part
of Elysium's kingdom
now that she is queen.

Lisa slides our drawings together,
holds them up beneath her desk lamp.
She pulls some tape from
the desk, sticks them to the wall.

She steps back
to look at the pictures,
puts her arm around my
shoulders. I feel the heavy,
perfect weight of her strong arm,
smooth against my neck,

and I feel the fire race through
to my toes. My body awake,
my back straight.
It's one of the first times
I realize that my stomach
isn't folding over my shorts as much.

She curls her arms up
into the air, flexing her muscles.
I am Elysium. The world is at my feet!
And there you are, her voice deep and
    silly,
a strong, mighty hunter!

Later, under the glow-in-the-dark stars,
when everything is quiet at last,
I unroll my bag
on the floor.
Lisa whispers,
    Good night, Ari,
    I'm glad you're here.
She points at her ceiling.
    We're like those stars,
    floating through the galaxy.
    You're like the brother
    I never knew I had.

Her words fold around me.

    Brother.
        Like a brother, a best friend.

        ....

I smile,
but I feel like it's
more than that.
I find the biggest star
in the center of the ceiling sky,
stare at it for a long time.
    I want to be more
    like two planets
    in orbit together.

I want to tell her this,
but by the time
I find the courage,
she's already asleep,
so instead I whisper,
    Good night,
coil in my sleeping bag
next to her bed,
watch the glow fade
from distant plastic stars.

A Different Kind of Morning

Lisa's mom has put out cereal boxes
and sits in the garden,
talking on her phone,
a book resting in her lap.
Lisa makes me scrambled eggs
with cheese without asking.

Gretchen just texted me.
Lisa smiles. *We're gonna meet her*

sometime this summer.
I think about Gretchen and Lisa.
I think about how
everything seems like a new chance.

My mother comes
shortly after we eat.
Her moccasins and work pants are absent,
her tank top and paint-drenched
canvas shirt
    missing.

She wears some kind of business suit,
gray over a white shirt, but still
with her silvery necklace.
I don't recognize the way she looks in it.
She hugs everyone, asks me standard
Did you? questions that all parents ask.
Did you have a good time?
Did you brush your teeth?
Did you get any sleep?
Did you keep to your diet?
Did you thank Lisa's mom?

I try to anchor myself to the next time
I get to see Lisa.
We hug, agree on *soon,*
and drive off toward the city.

Across the Golden Gate

The Golden Gate Bridge is enormous.
Its towers rise sentinel red
over the headlands,
into deep fog.

I just need to take care of some business
over the next week or so.
My mother tries to sound upbeat, for my sake.

I think of my father,
that he must have a plan,
that they are going to work it out.
After all, this isn't the first time
they've been so mad at each other.
Maybe he'll even be home
watching old shows,
like we always do.

I think of the rabbi's
methodical voice,
how I haven't been
to a Hebrew lesson in a month,
how whenever I mention anything
about it, my mother just says,
It's your father's job to deal with this.
I can't remember one prayer.
I try to think where the tape
of the rabbi speaking the prayers is.
I search my room in my mind.

....

Past the second tower,
I feel the heaviness of San Francisco,
invisible in a mass of swollen fog.

I think about Pick in Australia now.
I wish he was here.
I picture Jorge, alone at the beach.
I think about Lisa, the nursery,
sand on my feet, clay between my fingers,
my sleeping mat and pictures of robots taped all around it.

My old body melting away.
My white T-shirt, loose
over my middle.
My shorts that used to be tight
are so baggy that my legs
don't press against the seams at all.

We pass the Presidio, once an old army post,
huge artillery batteries turned into
living museums, and airstrips
restored into wetlands and grassy fields,
a huge park stretching all along the bay
green and alive in the wet air,
one of my favorite places
in the city.

We drive into the Marina,
past the long, low rows
of art deco houses
my mother always points out,
until we turn, at last,

to the street where
our apartment is.
Through the bay window,
I see the huge clay sculpture
of a woman's head
looking out at the street,
and it makes it feel
a little like home
     even though I feel so different.

Level 2: Ongoing Weight Loss

The first thing I do
when we get back
to our apartment
is weigh myself.

                                   21 pounds.

21 pounds less
than when I started.
I rest at the mirror again,
stare into an unfamiliar face.
Less chin now,
square jawbones,
the puffed slope
of my cheek
slides into
a less dimpled mouth.
I turn sideways,
suck in my belly.

There has never been
a time where I haven't held it in.

My love handles
rise over my shorts,
but they are smaller now,
barely enough to squeeze.

I go to the breakfast table.
It's just my mom and me.
Level two, she says. *It begins today*.
She sets down her copy
of *The Diet Book*,
dog-eared,
raises a cup of coffee at me in victory,
slides a bowl of cottage cheese,
and a pewter dish with twenty-four
      almonds.
I bite into halves
so they last longer.

Old Photo

My mother searches through
endless boxes of papers,
and finds an old photo
of a time in New York,
at P.S. 6,
where once I played
the part of a king
in a school play.
Other kids
wore cardboard armor
and swords made of tinfoil.

But as the king, I wore
a costume my proud parents rented me.
King Henry the Eighth,
red velour with golden trim,
white sheer tights expanded over my legs,
a crown, and even a real sword.

In the picture of that day,
my face is noble,
on top of too many chins,
my belly spilling over my gold belt.

This was the first time I noticed you were chubby.
How did that happen? she asks.

Me too. I noticed it then.
But not for the first time.

Stuck in the City

Alone,
my mom
off to deal with lawyers, clients, customers,
maybe even my father, I think,
but she doesn't say it.
It's a whole list I don't understand.
I have to leave early
and come home late every day this week, she says.

I live out Level 2 the best I can,
more carbohydrates than Level 1,

even a little sugar, but only from fruit.
I pour twenty-four almonds in a bowl,
grab a coffee cup of blueberries,
and roll a piece of salami tightly
with a slice of Swiss cheese.

I make it fancy on a plate,
pour a glass of diet soda.

I pass the tall mirror
in the hallway
to make sure the weight
didn't somehow come back.
I look at myself,
first straight on,
then I turn to my side,
suck it in,
      let out my breath

     because the weight is still gone.

I sit on the couch
and turn on the TV.
I eat almonds
and watch *Magnum P.I.*
on Netflix, like I do with my father.
We love to watch old shows together.
The actor's Hawaiian shirts
unbuttoned too far,
like my father's shirts.

Sometimes when we were back in New York,
my father sent me

to the market down the street
to get cupcakes and Hershey's bars,
and then we would
sit and eat them all,
him explaining
the plot of *Lost*,
or watching reruns of
Happy Days
or *Hill Street Blues*.

The couch feels good.
I've been away from couches
and TVs, computers, and *Magnum*,
and *Voltron*, and everything else.
When each new show starts,
I taste cupcakes and potato chips,
smell oatmeal cookies,
feel chocolate melting on my tongue.

I breathe,
      eat a blueberry instead.

Sardines

During these long days,
I sit sometimes
in the empty space
and wait for him,
the sound of his keys in the door
or the smell
of the sardines
he eats every day.

I walk to the kitchen
open the pantry door,
find cans of deviled ham
and uncut salami.
But on the third shelf,
just below the beanless
chili, the beef jerky,
I find
the tiny
star-shined tin
of sardines.
His sardines.
The ones he told
me were only for grown-ups.

I put it on the counter,
unhinge the lid
with the square key,
and slowly peel the metal back.
I stand in the kitchen.
I hear doors open and close.
I hear buses slip
and buzz along wires.
The kitchen
fills with a faraway sea.
I eat all the sardines
one by one
and lick
the tin
clean.

Atari

Once, in New York,
after many nights
of working late,
my father came home with
an old Atari 2600
tucked under his arm
and a brown paper bag
full of Atari games
and dumped them on my bed.
He unplugged my Nintendo,
pushed aside my Xbox,
and we stayed up all night
playing *Adventure* and *Breakout*
way past my bedtime.

But sometimes I waited,
and he didn't come home.

No Eyes on Me

I ride my bike to the bagel shop
my dad used to take me to.
When I get close,
I slow down,
look inside the window,
thinking he might be there
at the corner table
where we usually sit,
his coffee steaming
over his lox, eggs, and onions.

I ride my bike
across the city,
from the Marina,
over green Fort Mason,
down to the wharf.
I ride all the way
up Divisadero
to Haight Street
to the comic-book store.
I feel good.
The city is mine.

When I get home,
I pull a stack
of new comics
out of my backpack.
It's quiet. I look around.
I can almost hear
my father's voice
from the living room,
calling out, *Ari, you home?*
It's strange how suddenly
my parents decided they
could leave me by myself.

But I think I might be getting
the hang of it. Freedom.
Taking care of myself.
Creating my own life.
I stretch out on my bed,
my body a little tighter now,
skin against my muscles,

stomach flatter,
slow breathing.
No voices,
no fire to burn
or hands to dream
     of holding.
No trolls to carve
or stories to write
or gates to lock,
or trash to take out.

No giant terra-cotta
demon spirits, *Melinda*,
or angels or alien talismans,
no people up and down the streets
or beach sirens
or pounding waves.
No sleeping on a camping mat
beneath freshly painted murals.
Just moments
     with no eyes on me.

Grandma's Letter

At the mailbox,
I find a letter from my grandma.

A part of me imagines
that someday soon
I'll be back on the subway to Brooklyn,
eating too many
lemon-flavored Italian ices

and winding up in her apartment,
the cleanest place in all of Brooklyn.

I open the letter and
pull out a folded
piece of stationery,
blue flowers in the center,
laced over a faded
Star of David.
Behind the ten-dollar bill
are the words,
Ari, we love you.
We hope you are happy.
We hope you are skinny.

Skinny.
I can hear her thick accent
and the kindness in her voice
that doesn't mean to wound.

If I ever wrote a letter back, I might tell her
that I am, in fact, not skinny.
I am happy, and feeling more like myself.

I wonder how they remember me.
How even across a distance like this
she thinks of my size.

What If?

I want to talk to Lisa
about the letter.

I want to text her,
but I don't have a cell phone,
just this old landline.

But then I have a sudden thought:
What if things have changed?
What if Lisa already went back to the
     beach,
and she's hanging out with those older
     boys.
What if she and Jorge
went on some adventure
without me?
What if her mother
won't let her go back at all
and the nursery and the beach
break off in a great earthquake,
the trolls we made fall into turbulent
waves and grinding sand.

Middle of Level 2

I'm due after this week
to lose three more pounds,
but in the morning,
I feel like my stomach
is twice the size.

I walk to the mirror
in the hallway
and stand straight, then sideways.

....

Years of looking,
of seeing, or hearing
words about my body,
make it impossible
to see clearly.

I feel like I am suddenly
off track,
filling up
instead of deflating.

At the scale,
I imagine
24 pounds
of victory,
fat squashed away.
24 pounds
no longer
me.

I step on.

       Left foot.

              Right foot.

My eyes squint tightly.

        When I open them
                I lose
my breath.
          This can't be right.

21 pounds was the last time,
but now,
in the cool morning,
5 pounds have found
their way back to me.

16.
    16 pounds
since it all started.
        How could this happen?

I put my fingers
in the waistband.
I feel for the free air
between my body
and my belt.

                Still there.

I take my shirt off.
I look for the fat kid
in the mirror.
He's there and not there.

Indiscretion

In *The Diet Book*,
the doctor warns us to beware of indiscretions,
that we all make mistakes
from time to time.
After induction

in Level 1,
I taught my body
not to eat carbs.
Devour fat, body!
Eat the fat,
and that is what it did.

In Level 2, the body is adjusting
to its new ways of digesting.
It searches for fat,
a memory of Doritos
and Coke in a can.

The body gets mixed
up in Level 2.
Processes slow down
in the memory
of old food.

Carbs find their way in
as subtle suggestions,
a roll at dinner,
an extra handful of peanuts,
too much fruit,
or just the crust of a pizza.
Indiscretions.

I walk to my closet,
stare at my clothes.
Most are dark,
slimming, as my mother says.
Not a single horizontal stripe.

I promised myself
new clothes
at the end of the summer.
I will buy new jeans
and slim-fit shirts with stripes.

I feel my bones
loose inside my body.
I feel tightness in my pants
and the cling of my shirt.
My skin cells tingle
with every touch of fabric.
This has to be in my head.

On a website, I read about
what to do when the diet
stalls. It says,
Be good to yourself,
lower your carb intake,
shock your body,
starve it again.
Exercise.

I hold the book in my hands,
stare at the picture of the doctor on
        the cover.

Maybe he doesn't know everything.
How does being good to myself
mean I have to shock my body?
To starve it?
This can't be the only way.

By now the cover
is creased and dull.
I'm getting tired of it.
I close it, hard, and put it on the shelf.

I am being good to myself.

Post-its

On the wall
in the kitchen
near the window
on the bulletin board
there are yellow Post-its
written in parent handwriting,
like flags from
when life was normal.

Milk,
    work at three,
call grandmother,

and somewhere, in the far, far corner
are the words, written by my father,
Wednesday, July 25th, 4 p.m.
and the word **Rabbi**.

Today.

There is no one to see me take
the Post-it off the board,

no one to know or remember
that this appointment ever existed.

I look at the phone,
willing my father to call at this moment,
tell me to get moving,
but not this time.
No air-and-tear-filled speech
about how his rabbi was good to him,
even after all the bad things
he said he had done as a kid,
getting in fights, being late
to synagogue, and sometimes
even lying to his parents.
He told me that seeing the rabbi,
the gathering of my study papers,
my cassettes, tying my shoes
and combing my hair, the quiet walk,
the silvery touch of the mezuzah
entering the synagogue on my own,

all of it is   ritual.
Part of my story. Part of my becoming a man.

I hold the Post-it,
     alone
in the quiet apartment,
no one to tell me whether
to go or not.
Something, for once, seems up to me,
standing near the apple bowl,
yellow Post-it between my fingers

with the word **Rabbi**
in felt marker.

I look at the refrigerator.
I think about my father.
I think about my choices.
I think about who I am,
who I want to be.
I think about the beach
and Lisa
and how the world
feels so big sometimes.

If I leave now,
I might make it.

The Visit

I scrawl a note,
attach the Post-it,
so she can see the date.
I spread it on the counter,

Mom, back at 6.

I eat a Slim Jim,
a new Level 2 snack,
lock the door behind me.

The Marina is warm,
fogless in the late
afternoon, and I
pedal slowly

up Divisadero
and into Pacific Heights.

I don't know the words
by heart,
so I practice
the cadence
of the prayers
with my breath.

The rabbi's office
below his apartment
is dusty and dark.
I knock until the brass knob
turns, and he pulls me inside.
It smells like old sofas,
like chicken broth and frying pans,
like my uncle's house
on Long Island.

He asks me if I'm hungry.
I am, but I say no.
I've never been here without
        my father.

He sits down in his gray chair,
and he says my name the long way.

He looks at me through his glasses.

It's quiet
like thick curtains.

....

In this moment,
I feel his hands
cover mine.

He looks at me
like he sees something
that isn't supposed to be there.
Ari Rosensweig, he says, *how are you?*

I don't know how to answer him.
I want to tell him
that my mother is gone every day.
I want to tell him that my father left,
and I don't understand why.
I want to tell him that my heart is on fire over a girl.
I want to tell him that I'm trying so hard
to change my life.
I want to tell him that I can't do it.
I have friends, but I'm lonely.
I want to tell him that I don't understand these prayers.
I want to ask him if God is real, and why he cares about
    any of this.

but

I just say,   *Okay.*

He blinks. Smiles.

And your mother?

I tell him the truth,
that she's painting

and sculpting a lot,
she's very, very busy, and we're
spending a lot of time at Stinson Beach.

He asks me
about my father.

I wait. I let the silence slip through my fingers.

He left,   I blurt out.

The rabbi looks at me.
Without any words
he goes to his desk,
finds a bag of saltwater taffy,
walks over and sits
down next to me.
Silently, he puts two wrapped
pieces of blue taffy in my hand,
squeezes my shoulder, and says,
Let's begin.

When I Get Home

All the lights are on.
All the windows open.
The sound of Zamfir's pan flute
fills the apartment.
Zamfir, the Romanian pan flute player
who, my mom says,
is the greatest who ever lived.
When I hear his music,

I know my mom
has had an especially hard day.

She won't even talk to me.

The Truth

I went to see the rabbi today.
She smokes on the stairs
outside the kitchen door.
It was good, I say.
I walk to the counter,
find scrambled eggs,
bacon, sausage, a few grapes.
Breakfast for dinner?

Silence

    I was worried sick,
she says, looking down the street,
away from me—

    Damn it,
she shouts.
The words bounce
from window to window.
    Who
       do   you
                    think you are!
She stomps her foot,
then lurches forward,

leaning, bent over.
She coughs out of her throat,
fights for air.
She coughs,
tries to talk,
but her breath
devours her words.
I think of what to say,
but nothing comes
except the desire
to make
up a story
to make
her feel better,
but I don't want to lie, so I just wait.
    Until
she lifts her head,
opens her mouth,
sucks in the atmosphere.
The air races into her,
becomes fire in her belly,
forms one loud gasp,
    then

                releases,

                              into

                                      screams

     screams

                              screams

into some turbulent vortex
spinning, rising
higher and higher,

until she just
    stops.

In that moment,
I think she might somehow
evaporate,
a woman
all gone.

I didn't think
that she would worry.
I've been left to myself
so much.
She slowly turns
one leg at a time,
her frame bent,
the glass still vibrating.

I wasn't sure if I should go, Mom.
I won't go again.

          No,   she says, suddenly calm.
Her eyes are murky, exhausted.

I'm so sorry, Mom.
I won't go again, who cares
about this bar mitzvah anyway!
It's just something Dad wanted.
    I try my best
    to be on her side,
    even though I do care.

I would cry, she says,
　　but I have nothing left.
She puts her hand on my shoulder.
Her face quivering,
　　That wasn't meant for you,
　　my big man, she says.
　　　　　　Go see the rabbi.
　　　　　　This bar mitzvah
　　　　　　　　is important for all of us.
She looks me in the eyes.
I think of a million questions.
I don't ask any of them.
Then she pulls me into her.
　　You know I love you, she says.

　　　　I do know.

You're growing up so much. Her sobs turn into a laugh.
　　　　　I guess it's time to get you your own phone.

She puts her hands on my middle.
　　You are getting skinny! She coughs,
still crying off and on.
　　I have to get some sleep.
She walks toward her bedroom.

Oh. She turns, calming down a bit.

Sunday, I think.
　　　　　Sunday we can go back to the beach.

Calling Lisa

I call Lisa
to let her know
that Sunday we get to go back!
She doesn't answer,
and there is no voice mail.
I wish I could text her,
but whatever's
going on, I hope she's okay,
all the way over on the other side
of the Golden Gate Bridge.
I tell my mom
to call her mom,
but she doesn't answer either.
Maybe, she says, *we can stop
by on our way.*

Gretchen

I look for some graph paper
so I can finally work
on our game a little bit,
but I find Gretchen's number
in my backpack, pushed
between the jacket fold
of *Mysterious World.*
I dial the number.
Hello? she answers in her scratchy,
freckled voice. *Hello?*
Hello, I say. *This is Ari, um, Lisa's friend?*
I am so nervous.

I know who you are, she says.
She laughs immediately,
like my voice is the voice
she's been waiting for all morning.
I feel my body sit straighter,
my mind ease. We talk,
and it's good.
I can't stop talking.
I tell her about things
I did in these few days I've been here.
I tell her truth mixed with untruths.
I tell her about how my dad left.
Oh my god, she says. *I'm so sorry.*

I tell her other things.
I've been riding my bike
all the way to Pier 39,
over to the arcade.

I played some basketball
down by the Marina.

I bought a bunch of new comics.
Do you read comics? I ask.
No, she says, *but I want to.*

I don't tell her how much
I stare into the mirror,
guarding my body against
gaining any more weight back
or how I'm starting to wonder
if I have to stay on this diet forever.

....

When I stop talking,
her voice is a waterfall.
She tells me about how she thinks
in high school she might become an artist,
and how she is trading Quiet Riot for Prince.
because he's so *rad*.

Before we hang up,
she makes me promise
to call her back in a few days.

I promise, and then I ask her,
Have you talked to Lisa?
You totally like her, she says.
Gretchen laughs into the phone
and her laugh makes me laugh too.
Lisa's totally awesome,
but so am I.
Just wait till we meet.

August

Level 3

At the start of August,
I have lost almost
30 pounds.

All the biking and swimming
is changing me too.

The insides of my thighs
are a straight line
all the way to my knees,

but most of all,
when I see myself
in the mirror
or a store window,

I notice
my jaw,
smooth,
just one chin, my chin,
at the end,
where it's supposed to be.

My mother asks me
if I'm ready for Level 3.

I'm supposed to eat more carbs now.
I'm supposed to stress my body with food.
Test it.

Stress it?

I don't want to. I'm tired.

Berries
cherries
melons
orange
pear
a small banana

The book says I may soon experience *uncontrollable
        cravings.*
But I have come so far. How could it get any worse?

Mysterious World

There will always be things unknown and perhaps unknowable.
                                                    Arthur C. Clarke

I open up *Arthur C. Clarke's*
Mysterious World
and stare at the empty eyes of the crystal skull,
let myself walk through those deep corridors.

I want to be like Arthur C. Clarke,
a naturalist. I want to carry
a notebook and a camera,
travel the world unlocking
mysteries of Earth:
frogs and fish falling from the sky,
the Green Children from Woolpit,
who spoke a language
never heard before.
Like the travelers who
first discovered animals, fairy-tale monsters,
nunda, the king cheetah, the okapi,
the mountain gorilla.
I imagine my own expeditions traveling
to the deep Amazon, Kilimanjaro, Loch Ness,
or through the Himalayas.

In the introduction,
Clarke writes,

The universe is such a strange and wonderful place that reality will
always outrun the wildest imagination.

The letters are worn from my finger
passing through the words.
He reminds me that no matter what,
the one thing
that's not a lie,
is that mystery is real.

31

When I go back to the beach, I think,
I might even take off my shirt.
I practice in our apartment,
walk to the tall mirror in the hallway,
stare at the white tank top,
and slowly lift it off.

I try to unhunch my shoulders,
but they feel cemented
from years of
trying to be more compact.

This time, as I stand up,
my stomach
and my belly
sit firmly above
the button of my shorts.

When I lean my head forward,
I have one chin, and my legs
are thinner. I think I might
even be taller.

....

This doesn't look like me.
It can't be me.
I don't look like this,

normal.

What if I didn't weigh myself.
    Not now.
        Not ever again?

This can't be right,
to live like this,
scale to scale,
pound to pound,
forever?

I walk slowly to the bathroom,
eye the scale, and step
one foot in front of the other.
The tiny white stage,
an altar.
Hello, scale, I whisper,
and close my eyes
so the numbers have time
to settle. Before I open my eyes,
I tell myself a lie,
that *I don't care*,
but I push it away,
and instead I utter something
like a prayer.

I open my eyes,
see the number,

do the math in my head
of all the weight I have lost.

21

      16

               and now: 31.

I breathe,
step off.
Step on
right away
to make sure.
31. Thirty-one.

                      31.

31.

It feels good,

but then, for a moment,
I think about the 31.
Where does it all go,
so much weight
suddenly gone
from my body?
Inside, I can still feel it,
but it's different,
still a part of me,
but transformed,
    not heavy anymore,
        just weightless memories
                of the real me.

The Heaviest Water Is My Father

I go with my mother to do errands
in the morning, and we have breakfast
at the Chestnut Street Bar and Grill.
She says I can have one piece of toast,
but I don't. I don't feel like eating.
I'm tired of errands and meetings,
of always wondering what will happen.

I have one more meeting today. With a lawyer.
I look up from my eggs.
You look so different, she says.
I don't respond. She keeps talking.
The business is sold.
I just need to sign the papers today.
So, she changes the subject,
I have a new idea
for a series of drawings.
She pulls a pen from her purse,
sketches a perfect hand reaching down
from the sky onto a beach,
talks to me about
some ancient goddess,
some story about rebirth
and redemption.
I think this new work
will make the ground shake.

Why? I ask, annoyed. I can't take it anymore.

She looks at me, draws her napkin toward her. *Why?*
Yes, I say. *Why does it even matter?*

Sometimes it seems like the art
matters more than I do.
Maybe my dad isn't here
because he felt like this too.
I look down into my plate
then at her hand sketching on the napkin.
For once, I wish she would stop sketching.
    Stop,   I say, loud.
The man at the next table looks
up from his book.
She leans in, holds my hands
like I'm a little boy.
Mom, I groan, *stop*.

It's okay, Ari, she tries to soothe me.
Expression is everything.

I shake her hands off me,
stand up,
    throw down my napkin,
               my hands balled into fists.
In this moment
more than any other time,
I want my father.
I want HIM to explain this to me,
what it means to sell a business,
to leave your family.
I want concrete rules,
like D&D rules.
Roll this die and 16–20
is a hit.

....

Ari, she says, tries to calm me,
and I feel the people
in the restaurant looking.

I walk toward the door.
I want to rip the menus off the wall.
I want to feel ocean water on my face.
I want to be someplace quiet,
reading *Mysterious World*.
I want my father.

Where is he?
Does he care that she's selling the business?
How can he let all this happen?

Where was he when I was on the bike path?

I want him to know
that the time he told me about,
when he was a kid
and they called him Jewboy,
happened to me too.

I want to tell him
that I still
watch our
old shows on Netflix.

I want to tell him
that I went to see the rabbi
all by myself.
I sit down outside

on a bench near
the restaurant window.

When my mother comes,
she looks embarrassed, tired,
but she sits down on the bench
close to me.

It's then that I feel tears.
I can't stop them.

I think about how maybe
my father was the heaviest
part of me.

And now that he has drained
away, I feel less than who I am.

She pulls me
by my elbow
up and onto my feet.
I don't fight it.

When we reach our apartment
she puts her hand on my head.
Do you have your keys?
My breathing is slow now. Normal.
It's going to be okay, Ari.
I turn up the stairs.

I'll see you tonight!
Hey, why don't you call Lisa again?
See if she wants us to pick her up?

Okay, I say.
Mom? I say.
She turns.
She is looking toward the corner,
toward the buses speeding
off into the city.

Yes?

I want
        to talk
                to Dad.

She looks down.

I know, she says. *I know.*

Calling My Father

I call Lisa
to let her know
about Sunday,
        but there's still no answer.

I hang up, but my hand stays on the phone,
and in that moment,
I decide to call my father.

Why shouldn't I?
I am nervous to call him
so I grab *Mysterious World,*
so I can read and breathe first.

When I find my courage
to call,
the phone rings
and rings
and rings.

This voice mailbox is full.

I call again,
       but it's the same every time.

I Pack

more comics,
graph paper,
and a few new dice
for the game.
I stare at the cover of
The Diet Book and ask,

Where does it end, Doctor? Do I just do this forever,
until I waste away into nothing?
    What happens
       when I can't find myself
             anymore?

A Date

In the middle of packing,
I hear Gretchen's

voice in my head
and think about how fun it is
to talk to her,
about how she says she loves my voice,
how much I like hers,
how funny she is,
how I can listen to her without trying,
and how she hears what I say,
how we promised to meet
somewhere in East Bay,
some mall or maybe Telegraph Avenue in Berkeley,
where we can go to old record stores.

We haven't even met.
She doesn't know that I'm fat,
that I might
not look like I sound.

I call, and she starts talking right away.
She tells me about Duran Duran.
Before I know it, she's singing
"Hungry Like the Wolf,"
and she expects me to sing the low parts,
and I do, and we sing on the phone,
and it doesn't even feel weird.

Pretty soon she's telling me
about Lisa, how they knew each
other in elementary school,
before Lisa moved to Mill Valley.

Gretchen promises me again,
over and over,

that soon we'll meet.
I say, *Cool.*

When? she asks, suddenly serious.
When?
Yes, when?
I don't know,
I say, *but we can
make a date before summer's over. . . .*

Great! It's a date, she says.

Her words snap the spell,
and I remember that she's
never seen me before.

I'm kind of a big guy,
I tell her.
I always have been.

Okay, she says.

*I'm tall, way taller than
most girls I know,
sometimes they make fun of me.
And I have lots of freckles.*

We make plans to go to the record store for sure,
find the Prince album she's looking for.
I tell her that for my bar mitzvah
I might get a vintage record player.

Let's sing one more song! she says. *Prince!
Let's sing "Purple Rain."*

That song is rad.
I tell her it's rad.
We sing it until I hear her mom
telling her to get off the phone.

Missed

I look at the old note
on the bulletin board,
the Post-it hanging by one
sticky edge.
It reminds me
that I had another
appointment yesterday!
I didn't remember,
missed it by a whole day.
Knots in my stomach.
How could I let this happen?
It's over, I think.
I let him down.

The House Call

I sit in my room.
I should be packing,
but instead I'm
reading *Web of Spider-Man #1*.
Peter is thinking about how to tell Mary Jane
he wants to be a new kind of hero.
He doesn't want to think of the past anymore.
By the last page,

Peter's symbiotic alien suit
decides to detach itself from its host
and save Peter's life—one being
suddenly split into two.
I carefully slide the comic book
back into its Mylar bag.

A knock at the door startles me.

I look through the peephole.

    It's the rabbi!

I feel a rush of nervousness.

He must be here for my mother.

I open the door,
and the rabbi looks up.
It's about time.
Is your mother home?
The rabbi doesn't waste words.

I'm sweating and there's a long pause.
He looks around the apartment.

It feels like when I first saw
Mrs. Goldberg, my third-grade
teacher, at the candy store
on Lexington Avenue,
like she wasn't supposed
to be anywhere but in school.

         ....

He searches the apartment,
taking in everything he can,
then his eyes
come back to me
and he smiles.
Can I come in?

*Sure—I'm not really supposed
to let anyone in, though.*

He looks around the kitchen.
Do you want a glass of water?
I pour him the water,
and he takes a drink,
and for a while we talk about stairs.
Up and down, he says. *Always with this city.
Up and down.*

Then the rabbi sits
on the barstool
in the kitchen,
Tell me how you are, Ari.
I lean on the counter.
Good?

There is a universe
in the answer I don't give.

He stares at me,
waiting inside the silence.
I'm reading a great book, I say.
He lifts an eyebrow.
Can I show you?
He nods.

I find *Mysterious World,*
dust the cover off
and straighten the torn jacket.
It's by Arthur C. Clarke.
You know, he wrote 2001: A Space Odyssey?
He nods, raises his eyebrow,
maybe acknowledging, maybe not.
His eyebrow stays perched.

I hold it up
like a preschool teacher
and open to the first few pages.
The crystal skull stares
the rabbi in the face.
Words bubble out
of my mouth.

It's Aztec or maybe Mayan. Nobody knows for sure. Some people
        think it's fake.
They say the skulls can tell the future if you look through
        their eyes.

I hold up the fullest-color picture
of the skull.

This is my book, I say.
I read it every day.

The rabbi looks at the book.
Looks at me.
The book again.
He smiles.

And that's when I tell him everything:
Bigfoot, Loch Ness, the Jersey Devil.
I flip through the pages,
my fingers a tour guide,
walking backward through
sacred pages.
These are the Nazca lines, forms of animals miles and miles long.
They can be seen from space.
No one is sure how they got there.

And on like this, and the rabbi
is laughing now like my grandfather would,
nodding and pointing, and every now and then
looking up at me.

I tell him how so many things
are just unexplained.

Do you know? he says,
his hand sliding across the counter
to the container full of spatulas.
He pulls one out and holds it up.

Once, in the desert, Moses
and his brother, they were in trouble.
They needed water,
so they begged for a miracle.
So he was given a staff
and told by Hashem to speak to a rock.

A rock! So do you think he
would go in front of all

those people and speak to a rock,
like he was supposed to do?
Would you, Ari? Talk to a rock?

No.

So he hit the rock instead,
because he was mad. Frustrated.
Have you ever wanted to hit something?
You know, when you are frustrated?

Well, you know what? Water came out, just like
he was promised, and all
those people got what they needed.
To them it was all a mystery:
a desert, a rock, then water
flowing through the tents,
children playing, animals drinking,
who knows. Unexplainable.

Moses, though, he knew better.
He did what he thought he had
to do to be the leader.
He knew the directions
but didn't trust to simply follow them:

Speak. Not hit.
Don't get mad,
trust the miracle
that he'd already
been given,
not bring doubt into it
or get frustrated because it's

not the way he wanted it to happen,
or just to look strong or smart,
like he thought everyone else wanted him to.

So even though everyone else drank,
he didn't get to drink at all.

Maybe, the rabbi says,
it's as simple
as believing that
you don't have to be
what others want you to be.

You can do the right thing
because your life
is already a miracle.

His voice glides through his beard.

I want to see you, Ari,
on your birthday. Do your
best to remember all you can.
Practice the prayers. Come see me.
We can get through this together.

He takes my hand,
rests his other hand
on top of *Mysterious World.*
This is a good book of mysteries.

Then he places a worn book on the counter,
the pages folded, strands of leather
hanging out.

This is also a book of mysteries.
I spend my life with it.
We are alike, Ari. You with your book,
me with mine. Let's share these.

I am here, Ari,
if you want to call me,
if you want to tell me about Bigfeet,
or when you go to Muir Woods,
or little green men,
or you find something strange.

He lifts *The Diet Book*
off the counter,
looks at it, eyebrows raised,
pointed. He speaks without
looking away.
Whatever you are trying so hard to do
on the outside,
it's who you are becoming
on the inside
that really matters.

You came to me without
anyone telling you to.
You let me in without
anyone forcing you.
    That's strength.
And here we are.
    I'm proud of you.

When he finally lets go of my hand,
I half expect to see saltwater taffy.
But it's just my hand and his freckled fingers.

He looks one more time at *Mysterious World*.
It's a good book!
he announces.
He takes a sip of water,
and he walks slowly toward the door.

I got to be going.
Be good to your mother.

He looks around one more time,
mutters something under his breath
and looks back at me,
then disappears down the stairs.

Finally

Packed,
    in the car,
        we cross the bridge,

drive through Mill Valley,
because I convince my mom
that we should at least
go by her house to check on her.

She texts her. No response.

No one is home.
My mom calls her mom.
No answer. Her mailbox is full.

We drive next to the bike path,
through town. The bakery is closed,

and I imagine marzipan potatoes
like a small pouch of sand
in my palm.

Before, I could've
eaten five in a row,
but now I think
one would be just perfect.

Homecoming

We wind our way
along the back roads to Stinson,
past old bunkers
of the Marin Headlands,
and the Marine Mammal Center.
    Winding all the way
around to Muir Beach
and back
down the twisted road
into Stinson, nestled
between the hills and the sea.

We open the nursery gate, and the courtyard
is filled with its terra-cotta citizens;
trolls, and plaster bodies, birds, and insects
welcome us back.

It's a homecoming my mother desperately needs,
and I see her with her face to the sun,
her silver hair translucent,
her face smooth and warm
in the afternoon light.

Settling (Back) In

Happy to be back at last,
I sit at the driftwood table
behind the counter,
lay out a half block of clay,
and three wood carving tools
in different sizes,
double wire,
single hook,
and straight spike.

I put the clay
on a paper plate,
tear off a piece,
and begin slapping it
against the ocean-soaked wood
with all my might
until the air
is all the way out.

I carve the trolls,
one round with stringy
coiled hair and sunken eyes.
The other tall and skinny,
with a sausage nose and a single
fang on the bottom lip,
then tiny, bulbous eyes
rolled between palms
and poked with the edge
of a toothpick.
Trolls on bikes
and boogie boards,

and with hiking sticks,
tiny backpacks,
and beach balls.

I let them dry
on the plate
in the warm sun.

Giant Salamander

Jorge sits at the bus stop
across the street.
His pencil furious
in his sketchbook.
A canvas bag full of groceries
at his feet.

Jorge! I call,
and he stands up.

Ari! he shouts.
I run across the street.
He holds up his sketchbook.

Look what I drew!
On the page,
is a picture of a pond.
At the bottom is
a massive lizard
with a line drawn across the edge
of the page: nine feet.

....

A giant salamander? ·

Yes, Jorge says. *This is one animal*
I think your book got right.
I think I saw one of these once.

I smile.

You guys are back? Jorge says.

Yes, I say. *We got back today.*

He looks toward the beach,

I thought you guys got back yesterday
because I saw Lisa in town.

Her name startles me. *Lisa?*
Yeah, he says. *I saw her earlier.*

She's at the beach right now.

I feel heavy and light at the same time.

Ari, he says, *it's weird.*
Remember that guy who gave us a hard time?
The one with the dark hair?
She's down there with him.

The bus pulls up.

I gotta go, but I'll call you later.
He hurries onto the bus,

his groceries and sketch pad
bundled together.

Glad you're back! he shouts.

I walk toward the beach.

The Surprise

Lisa says
that at least once a day
you have to put your feet
in the ocean.

I walk down to the beach.
The waves are big and far away,
breaking way offshore,
red flags along the beach
warning everyone
of heavy surf.

I walk toward the water,
past the SHARK ADVISORY signs,
past the gray lifeguard tower.
There are a few people
in our usual spot,
some kids chasing
an orange Frisbee,
and a couple sitting close together.

That's when I notice it,
the black backpack

with the Def Leppard patch.
    Her blond hair

              down her back,

maybe a little wet,
the hints of her blue bikini
against her perfect browned skin,
her behind nestled into the sand,
sitting with arms over her knees.

She leans slightly into the boy.
Older, muscular, rounded shoulders,
his arm around *her* waist
dug in the sand.
He whispers something to her,
looks off to the ocean.
It doesn't take long
to recognize him.
I can still hear
the voice of his friend
in my mind. *Baby Huey's got a girrrlfriend. . . .*

How is she here?

                         How is she with him?

How does everything

become nothing
                in such a short time?

I feel my stomach
fall into the sand.

I pick it up,
look at it,
hold it up to the sun.
It's sandy but
completely transparent,
suddenly empty.
I hold my heart too,
beating wildly like
my chest might actually
explode.

I back into the tree line
step by step.

I am so far away
from what I understand.

Not Dealing

In the evening,
back at the nursery,
Lisa finally walks
through the gate.

Hey, Ari!

she calls,
            and runs over to hug me.

            I don't give it back.

You're getting taller, Ari,
but you're smaller too.
I'm not used to my arms
reaching all around you!

My heart beats.
I feel the faded bruise on my side throb twice,
one sharp pain and then a low, blunt beat.

Only Child

I want to be excited to see her.
I missed my friend.

She's only
a few feet away
on her sleeping mat,
and we haven't even
talked about how she
got out here
before us.

It's okay, I think.
I'm *used* to being alone,
an only child,
left to myself.

I'm good at it.

At P.S. 6,
the teachers always told
my parents that I was

excellent at dealing
with teasing from other kids.

Maybe I can be tough.

Boogie Boarding

When the sun comes up,
I sit outside near *Melinda*.
Lisa calls out from the main room,
Wanna go boogie boarding?
    Sure. Fine.
We get the boards,
shake off the old sand.
Mine is deep blue with
a rainbow swirl on the back,
and hers is also blue with a pink sheen.
The leashes spread and fray,
too much sun, too much salt.

It's early enough,
quiet, and the sculptures
in the garden watch us open the gate
and slip through the fence.

What do you think the surf will be like? she asks.
It will probably suck, I answer.

She sighs at me.

I look over at her.
Her hair is messed up in the back.
I love how she never wears any makeup.

We should try to ride the waves together.
Remember how we did it a few times ago?
One-two-three gooo! And then I always beat you to shore.
She's trying so hard.

I don't say anything,
stare straight ahead.
I feel her shoulder bump into my shoulder.
Stop it, I say. She looks at me.
How long are you gonna act like this?
She taps my boogie board with her foot.
Do you want to talk about it?
About what? I lash out at her.
That you didn't even call me?
Not once?

She leaves it there,
knows better.

We get to the beach.
There's no one in the water.
Everyone stands in the sand,
and the lifeguards go up and down
the beach with megaphones,
holding boards
with a picture of a shark.
A great white was seen off the coast
early in the morning.

We pass the lifeguard tower,
stand there with our boards dug in
and our feet curling deep
into the warmth of the sand.

A Drive

Do you want to go for a drive?
Mom asks.
Just you and me.

I don't, but I go anyway.

We drive
Shoreline Highway
toward Bolinas,
pass Seadrift
near the Audubon Canyon Ranch.

Water is coming.
Deep saltwater rivers
flow into the lagoon
where mudflats disappear
into clear glass.
       Coots and cormorants
                    sweep from the sky,
drop into the water
       come back with beaks full of bluegill.

I see Kent Island,
where the mother seals
are shiny duffel bags
on the beach.
Their pups
scoot into the water,
their half-circle heads
with giant, deep eyes
pop and peek over
wakes they make.

. . . .

I want so badly
to swim out
to Seal Island,
walk on the shore,
and just sit in the middle of them,
their round bodies
fat on purpose
to keep warm
in the cool water.

In Bolinas,
we park near the general store,
walk along the giant wall murals,

     multicolored hands intertwined, sun on fire,
     green turtles and redwood beetles,
     a mountain lion and mermaid.

Do you want to get ice cream, Ari?
Her question surprises me,
but when I look at her,
I see she's trying to cheer me up,
share something together
like we've always done.

               I do.

Vanilla-filled sugar cones
dipped in chocolate,
the kind where the shell
hardens and cracks in a second.

We eat it by the water.

Plans

Jorge calls,
and we make plans
for our hike.

Do you want to go overnight?

I think about it. Scared a little,
but it's perfect timing,
a chance to get away,
have an adventure.

Yes.

We agree to check
with our moms.

The Mothers Talk

I wait until after breakfast,
when she's had her coffee,
opened the doors,
and begun to swirl the paint.

Mom, Jorge and me,
we want to hike up Bolinas Ridge.
Tomorrow?

She stops swirling, smiles at me.
Can I go, Mom? By ourselves?
It's an overnight.

You just have to take us up the road
near Olema, and then we take
McCurdy Trail to Bolinas Ridge.
There's a campground
near the top. (There isn't.)

Jorge has a phone,
so we can tell you how we are. (He does.)

She pulls out her phone,
calls Jorge's mom.

In the corner of the nursery,
near the door,
a gray mouse makes a break for it.
It scurries across the floor,
pauses by the doorframe,
and lifts its front paws in the air,
then down into a crack
in the old wooden deck.

I hear chatter on either
side of the call,
the sounds of mothers talking
in secret languages,
a thousand words that lead to

Yes

Tools for the Journey

Jorge comes over the next morning
like some adventurer

on his way to Middle-earth
or some other fantasy world.
He opens his sketchbook,
pours out maps he's made,
shows me notes on trees
and poison oak.
He turns the pages slowly,
explains each drawing,

his giant hands in all directions
like some kind of minister.

Lisa walks in.
Jorge puts his hand
on her shoulder.
Lisa, you should come with us!
And he smiles an irresistible smile.
Where? she asks.
Her hair pulled back.
No makeup. Beautiful.
She sits down.
Jorge explains the trip,
tapping his carved wooden cross
from fingertips to palm,
occasionally looking at me.

Not Telling

I avoid her,
walk toward the counter,
drink some water,
pretend to pack.

Lisa walks over to me.
You don't want me to go?
I say nothing.
Ari?

I look up
at her impossible face.
It's so hard to stay angry.
I don't care.
I tighten my body,
shrug my shoulders,
feel my belly burn.

    I know you're mad.
She is a magnet,
I am metal,
resisting.

I am mad!

Jorge looks over,
then walks toward the gate
and just outside.

I pluck my words from my
mouth one by one,
put them in the air around her.
How could you? With him?
Why?
Why didn't you call me?
Where were you?
How did you get out here?

Weren't you even
wondering what was happening
to me?
I called you!

I pause. She looks at me,
her eyes fixed.

My dad left,
and I was all alone.
All the time. Alone.

And in her green eyes,
staring at me,
I see for a second
a reflection
of my own body,
distorted and turned
inside out.
It's not her fault
or mine.

I feel my side ache.
I put my hand there,
and she puts her hand there too,
softly over mine.
Her strong fingers
intertwine,
and with her other hand
she moves my hair away from my eyes.

My feet are nailed to the wood
floor, my heart slow and heavy,

quiet now
my eyes soaked
and she's so close
I feel her breath
I'm in her orbit
circling closer
in in in.

In some other dimension,
the other me is brave,
but here, this me
coughs a little,
suddenly thinks about
how his bent head
might be pushing his chin
just a little too much
into a double chin,
or that he'd better pull his pants up.

This me, angry, ashamed,
turns his head,
breathes her in,
and walks away.

Packing List

1 sleeping bag
1 bottle of water
1 package diet Hawaiian Punch powder
1 military shovel
1 Rambo-style survival knife
    with twisting compass on the hilt

and a hollow compartment in the handle
Inside: matches, a sharpening stone.
1 bag of dehydrated ice cream
2 bags of brand-name pork rinds
2 packs of Budding roast beef
1 small bag of shredded cheese
2 apples
1 small bag of sugar-free jelly beans
1 sketch pad, graph paper
2 pencils
1 pen
2 pairs of socks, both with blue stripes
1 pair of underwear
1 long-sleeved T-shirt with the California flag
1 *Diet Book*
1 *Mysterious World*

One note folded tightly
taped to three Slim Jims
that I find later that day.

Dear Ari,
Have a great trip.
I know you and Jorge
will be safe.
I thought you might
need these Slim Jims?
I want you to know
that you are such
a good friend to me.
I am sorry if I
hurt your feelings.

I will try to be brave
  in the waves
    without you!
      Elysium.

Fog Storm

On the way to the trailhead,
fog swallows the whole road.

Shoreline Highway
two miles past Dogtown,
a huge deer cuts across the road.
My mother swerves. Already hard to see.

She slowly winds
along the road
then announces,
like a final warning
or a chance to turn back,

They say that this
will be the worst fog
in a hundred years.
Are you kids sure about this?
It might even rain?
In the middle of summer!

When we reach the trailhead,
we burst from the car.
Lean our packs against

the wooden sign,
the gateway to Bolinas Ridge.

She hugs us both,
and she waits outside the car,
her cigarette smoke
polluting the wet air
as the fog thickens.
Somehow, she knows
we have to do this.

See you tomorrow,
she says.
Be careful.

Up the Trail

Up.
    The fog gets thicker,
and the ground is still
summer-baked earth,
and sliding feet,
ankles turning over gravel,
our packs ten times too heavy.

Finally,
at one of the turns
where we curve
around what we think
is the top of the trail
at last, we see the trees

rise out of the fog
until finally we reach
the spine of the mountain.

Flat. Trees.
BOLINAS RIDGE
        at last.
Redwoods soar across the trail.
The Pacific spreads
into an endless blue horizon.
We seem so far from the bottom.

Jorge takes off his pack
near a wood sign
where the trails split.
My back is drenched
with sweat and wet air,
my feet wet too.
My legs ache.
I don't think I've ever
pushed my body
this much before.
I feel my breath,
but I can't slow it down,
my heart beating
way too fast.

Outdoor Conversations

Do you like her? Jorge asks.
Who? I say. But I know who.

Lisa. I mean it seems like you do.
I love her, I say. *You know,*
like a sister, I mean.

But what if I do?
What if this
is what love feels like?

Do you see that? I ask.
I point to a dark shape in the sky.
A bird soars, black against the gray fog.
I reach into my backpack,
pull out *Mysterious World,*
start to flip through its pages.
There are so many giant birds
in mythology that appear
when there are storms or fog.
But then I remember something
and I stop, close the book.
I think about how when I was little,
my father loved taking me
to Central Park on Sunday mornings
to look for birds.
   I wish he could see this one.

Jorge, I say,
where's your dad?
I don't know, he says
between breaths.
I never met him.

Campsite

We hike along the ridge for a while.
The trees rise and fall over the edges of the trail,
toward the coast,
a blanket of green.

We walk
until we find the spot
where the trees are so thick
that every direction looks the same,
and we fold into the forest.

Jorge finds a deer trail,
a tiny path, barely noticeable
through the thick ferns and bushes.
We follow it down
toward the valley,
our legs scraping
against rocks and bushes,
the sun dropping
while more fog rolls in.

We come to a clearing
with four boulders
like moss-covered
gnome houses
in a half circle,
a miniature Stonehenge.

We should camp here, Jorge says.

....

We unroll our packs.
I follow Jorge,
do what he does.

      a.   Gather wood.
      b.   Put small rocks in a circle for the fire between us.
      c.   Clear brush.
      d.   Use a tarp. The ground will be wet tonight.
      e.   Keep watch.

               Then, quietly, I whisper the Shema, a
declaration of faith . . . as much as I can remember.

Roasted Hot Dogs

Jorge tells me to gather wood,
so I fill my arms
with sticks of all sizes.
Near an old log,
I step into a spring.
It's covered in leaves,
hard to see,
and my feet
are soaked with mud.
When I wander back,
I see that he's gathered at least
fifteen times my load.
He makes the sticks into a small tepee,
tells me to get matches,
and I pull out the big box from my pack,
strike one. *Not yet!* he says.

....

light
blow
fail

again until it works.

The orange fire rises in the dimness
of the evening coming on.
Trees fade into the sky,
the boulders illuminated in orange and yellow.

Starving,

we stretch long wire hangers
and roast hot dogs
until they are a little burned.
Jorge slides his into slices of bread;
I eat mine right off the hanger.

I put my feet near the fire,
but they can't seem to get dry or warm.

Crush

Tell me about this diet, Jorge says.
It's the first time he's asked me.
In the orange fog,
I tell him about all of it,
growing up in New York,
always being overweight.
I list the names I've been called
and how I had to talk to all those doctors.

It's sort of funny now when I say it to him, and we
      laugh.
Then we're silent when I tell him about the bike path,
and about hurting myself,
and *The Diet Book.*
About Lisa,
about my father.

Later,
I eat celery stuffed with peanut butter (Level 3),
and Jorge burns marshmallows.

I think I do like her, I confess.
Like a crush?
Yeah, I say, *I guess.*
I forget sometimes,
because Jorge is so tall,
that he's younger than us.
I don't have a crush,
Jorge says. *What's it feel like?*
I point at the fire with my
celery stick. *Like that.*
Like fire. All over the place,
it feels good from far away,
but you can't really get near it.

Prayers

By the time we finish talking,
we are in our sleeping bags,
near the edge of the slowly ending fire.

Jorge puts his carved wooden cross
next to his sleeping bag.

My feet are freezing,
and my head aches
from so much walking.
I try to get warm inside my bag,
but it isn't working.
Can you say a prayer for me too? I whisper.
He does.

Visitors

The last embers
of the fire float up into
the starless sky,
and then, suddenly, one by one,
dark shapes skulk out of the fog,
long necks and stretched bodies
step slowly through the boulders,
quiet barks and grunts
from their low-hanging heads.
I hold my breath,
hide my head in my bag.
It's a family of Sasquatch, or forest goblins.
This can't be real.
    I unzip my bag
      just enough to feel
      the sudden breath on my face,
      of an unexpected monster,
      a Tule elk above me,

his huge muzzle smelling me
from head to toe.

I've never felt so small in my life.

We stare at each other for a long time,
and I can see myself in his eyes
until he softly grunts, his eyes aglow
in the dying firelight, and moves on.

I watch them disappear,
one by one
in the dying firelight,
their bodies silent,
into the deep woods.

Hypothermia

When we wake up,
my feet are numb,
my head soaked,
and I can't stop shivering
no matter what I do.
Let's get going,
Jorge says.
It will warm us up.
So we pack everything
and start hiking,
my hands shivering,
my feet aching
in this impossible cold.
My head starts to feel

like fog is swirling
around on the inside.

Down the trail,
I start to see strange things,
like when you first
close your eyes before bed:
trees taking steps,
long arms and claws,
sometimes leaning over,
turning as we walk by,
giants in the mist.

My wet feet squish with every step,
my body so tired. I just want to stop.

Jorge is way ahead by now.
I see his blue backpack
turn a corner
on the windy trail,
sucked away
into the fog.

One
    step
            at
                    a
                                  time.

Have courage.

I can't catch up.
I can't see Jorge.

I yell out.
How did he get so far away?

I can't see past
the length of my arms.
My feet squish raw
in my soaked shoes.

Walk   Walk
        Walk   until I'm exhausted.

Stop.

                        Along the trail,
                        a giant moss-covered boulder
                        sits alone at a gentle turn.

                        Sit with me, it says.

I should have eaten more.
Not enough water?
My head is aching,
pounding. I'm so tired,
shivering still.

I decide to listen to the rock,
feel my muscles melt
into moss and granite.
I look at my calculator watch,
but the numbers
are far away, and

my hands are shaking.
　　　　　How far have we gone?
　　　　　　　　　Where is Jorge?

I can't feel my feet.
　　I want to lie down

　　　　　　in this bed
　　　　　　　　　of horsetail ferns
　　　　　　　　　　　　and short moss,
where a thousand ladybugs
swirl in an old log.
It's so quiet.
　　Finally quiet.
　　　　I could sleep. Sleep.

Things That Exist

Ari?

Is it the rock talking?
I spread my fingers
on the cool moss.
Ari, the voice through the fog and forest.

Arrriii!

It's Jorge.
Are you okay?
He puts his hand on my shoulder.

Sorry, I got lost too. You wandered
over here,
way off the trail.

Jorge takes off my shoes
and socks.
My . . . my feet, I say.
I can barely feel them.
He pulls a dry towel
out of his backpack
and wraps it tightly
around my feet.
My eyes open
wide, and my body
explodes into one icy shiver.

Then, suddenly,
the sun is coming out,
finding me through the trees,
and my head starts to clear.

Jorge talks to me
about hypothermia.
Are you okay, Ari?
You have every symptom.
Do you remember who you are?

I am okay.

But I feel different,
like the island
in the lagoon.

It's meant to be
where it is.

There are things
that are true,
no matter what.

My body changing,
Mysterious World,
friendship,
trolls in the gallery,
boogie boards,
sleeping mats,
late-night laughing.
Lisa. Pick.
Gretchen.
Elysium,
drawings,
trees,
the ocean,
the voice of the rabbi
reciting scripture,

> *Hope in the Lord. Strength renewed. Soar on wings like*
> *eagles;*
> *run and not grow weary, walk and not be faint.*

All of this is real.
                    All of this brings me back,

     still exists.

We eat almonds
and sugar-free jelly beans,

until my legs
aren't numb anymore.

Mikveh

We walk in the bright sun.
Coastal oak and redwoods
are earth brown and emerald green,
grass and trees,
boulders and ferns,
this unexpected foggy summer
has watered the valley
into furious growth.

We look back
toward the main trail.
If we walked up now,
we could turn and go right down
the hill to the bus stop in a few hours.

Jorge holds up his sketchbook
like he's reading an ancient chart.
This forest is not on my map.
We decide to keep going.
Down and down,
we slip away from the main trail
and finally to a pond,
blue crystal
and water glass.
It's more like a pool
spilling out into tiny streams
across the valley.

I heard these places are out here,
Jorge whispers,
but I've never
seen this before.

Look at that! Jorge shouts.
A giant black bird flies across
the valley, too big to be a crow.
We watch it circle over the water,
then directly over us.

We lay our stuff on a boulder
near the water, take off our drenched
shoes and socks, and lay them across
the dry rock.
My feet finally warm in the sun.
We stretch our bodies
along the banks of the pond,

dip our hands
into the cool of the water,
splash it on our faces.

I watch my reflection
watch me.

I'm not who I once was.

I know all of my reflections:
the mirror in our San Francisco apartment
has one swerve in the glass that widens
what it sees.

At the Dolan house, the mirror
is hung too high,
so there's only time for faces.

Lisa has a full-length
mirror in her room
that captures everything.

The bathroom mirror in the nursery
is giant and warped
and falling apart.

But there's no fear
in *this* reflection,
just trees, glassy water,
a different me
against a bright-blue sky.

The more I look,
the more I think about who I see.
Just maybe
    for the first time
        I don't *overlook*
or try to get away.
    I don't have to be my father

        or perfect for Lisa

            or anyone else.

Be myself.

....

Myself is okay.

I want this feeling to stay.
I want to know
that the next time
I look into those mirrors
this is the me I will see.

I take a breath, then
dunk my whole head into the pond.
I stay as long as I can.
    Come up and take
        another gulping breath.

Jorge! I say. *The rabbi told me*
that when I dunk myself in the water
and say certain prayers, it's a mikveh.
It's supposed to mean
I made a big change!
And then, more quietly,
    Do you think I have?

He laughs and nods. He's excited.
It's called baptism! he yells
and walks over to where water
is coming out of my nose,
and I am coughing
and trying to talk all at once.

He pulls out his own little trinkets,
a map, his wooden cross,

a small vial, a smooth river
rock with the word *faith*
painted in white,
his sketchbook,
and two long pencils,
and sits next to me near the water.

On either side of the valley,
the trees flow down like
the river water.
I want to swim in the pond,
maybe go all the way under.
I take off my shirt.
I feel the air and the sun
on my skin.

It's cold, Jorge says, already wading in the water.
I know, I say, *but I've been wet all night
and all morning anyway.*

I smile and look back.
Jorge smiles,
begins to say prayers.
I don't know the prayers
for what I would say,
so I just listen,
say something in my mind to God.
When I think of God, I imagine the rabbi
telling me that *I can do it*,
that I already have.

I go in,
watch my reflection

in the water,
try to find the image
of the fat kid
staring back at me,
but this time it's different.
    It's just the water that widens me.
I don't see a fat kid,
     not anymore.
        I simply
            see
               myself.
I go deeper
beneath the pond water
until my breath has given
everything it has
and my face
    breaks the surface
       into sunlight and air.

Resting Place

I stretch out on the boulder

shivering, trying
to dry out in the sun.
Maybe that wasn't the best idea?
We laugh.

I grab the last
of my beef jerky
from my backpack,
pull out

The Diet Book.
I need to look up
how many apples I can have.

Somewhere between
the jerky going into my mouth
and my body flipping over
to lie on my stomach,
the book
    slips
        from my hands,

bounces once
        on the far side of the rock,
then down
    directly
        into the sudden
                depth of the pond.

I watch it drop
into the water,
the yellowed pages
curling over each other,
trying to swim up,
keep it from drowning.
The letters
come off the pages,
float up,
disappear
at the surface
        Ketosi . . .

    Heavy Cre . . . carb . . .

Ba c n an   Eg ... imag i e ... los ng ... we g t ...

I think about
going after it.
  Fish it out,
  dry it off,
  start again.

                                    But I don't.

I leave it there.
A few feet underwater.
The doctor still smiling.
Thanks, I say,
but I've got this.

Its yellow cover
fading in its watery
resting place.

The Way Back

When we see the ocean,
we run along the open path
beneath the bright-blue sky.
Hikers take heavy steps up,
families, little boys and girls,
and all kinds of dogs.
Yesterday we were alone.
Today the trails are filled with people,
each climbing into something different.

I feel lighter,
like the change on the outside of my body
and the change on the inside have finally met.

At the base of the trail,
past the parking lot,
we see the simple blue-green picture of a bus,
the number 61, that will take us back.

End of Summer

It feels good to sit,
rock back and forth
in bus rhythm
along Shoreline Highway.

Jorge draws quietly in his sketchbook
as I tell him more about the game
me and Pick are making.

We feel the heaviness of late August,
and as we near the turn into Bolinas,
I understand that this might be our last week.

I have to go to school in Mill Valley.
I tell him about my school,
and what I think it might be like
now that so much has changed.

He looks at me. Smiles.
I hope you don't change too much.

He draws a hand coming
out of the center of the lake,
and in the hand is a long silver sword.

The 61 bus circles into town.
It's his stop.
Jorge puts his hand on my shoulder,
tears out the picture of the lake,
hands it to me. *Bye*, he says.
Later, I say, and he heads off the bus.

The bus drives,
along the lagoon,
past Seal Island,
where pups surface
near the shore,
    getting braver,
down past the houses,

to the last stop in the town.

The Return

I get off the bus,
my pack heavy,
my shoes untied.

I see myself in the window
of a truck as I walk by.
The window makes me look
twice my width,

my legs thick,
my face doubled,
covered in dirt.

At the nursery,
the wide gate is open.
I can see lights
strung up, and some colorful flags.
Zamfir is playing,
the pan flute wailing out of the gate.
People wander through the nursery
drinking champagne.

Lisa is there.
She's holding a paintbrush
and standing next to an oil painting
on an easel.
She sees me.

I imagine for a split second
that I'm the lost adventurer
scruffy and worn from the trail.
I am tough, distant and hard to reach
even for her.

In the next second,
I imagine I am as wide as
the truck-window me.
Awkward and waddling in.

Before I decide who I actually am,
she smiles, runs over,
throws her arms around me.

....

I feel every
    single
        part of her
            against my body.

Well? she says. *How was it?*
And in this moment,
I remember just how much
I miss her, and I explode
about the whole trip.
We step back in time.
Brother and sister,
best friends, as the confusing parts of me
shut off long enough to remember
that I don't have to be mad at her,
that with her I can just be me.

The Painting

What is this? I ask,
and I walk to where
the new painting rests
on the easel.
Oil and acrylic
in earthy tones,
            a woman
with claws
sitting beneath
a full moon,
crouched,
her legs
alive in fiery muscle,

barefoot,
her dark eyes
animal,
deep brown,
fierce but thoughtful.
Beneath her feet
the words
Deer Woman, eyes open.
        It's called a mara, *Lisa says,*
a Deer Woman, kind of.
I read these lines in a poem.
A mara's *like a werewolf*
in Sweden.

Lisa's painting is so different
from anything else here,
like a part of Lisa
I knew was there all along,
but didn't quite
recognize until now.
Your mom and me, well,
she's been showing me how
to work in texture, and . . .
*I've learned so—*I cut her off.
It's you! I say.
I mean if you were
a Swedish werewolf creature.

Sorry

The Artist comes outside,
a glass of champagne in one hand,

a long cigarette in the other.
I'm not sure if she'll be mad
at me for not calling,
or if she's been worrying about us.
If I tell her about almost
getting hypothermia,
or dropping *The Diet Book*
in the water or any of the other stuff,
she may never let me do anything again.

I take a deep breath, smile nervously,
Hi, Mom, I say through the crowd.
She stops suddenly,
      walks over
            looks me straight in the eyes
                  like she's reading my mind,
   then hugs me extralong.

Ari, she says,
tell me everything.

I'm tired, I say,
and she agrees and says that
later she'll make some Level 3 food,
even some bread tonight.
She walks off to greet guests.

Lisa pinches my arm.
Do you want to walk down to the beach?
Okay, I say. Even though I am so tired.
   This is what we do.
We go to the beach.

On the way there,
she takes my hand,
and then she smacks
her shoulder into mine,
and I do it back.

She asks,
*So what would Thall
and Elysium do right now?*

I tell her they would most likely
take over this defenseless town.
She agrees and pulls
an air sword from her side.
Onward, she says.

When we get to the beach,
her sword shimmers red
in the sunset,
and our feet dig into the sand.
My heart is beating faster,
and Lisa can feel it.
Are you okay? she asks.
Sorry, I say.
You always say sorry.
You know you don't have to be.
I'm the one who should be sorry.
I should be a better friend.

Something Takes Over

I think about what
I just went through,
the night on the mountain,
the wet, the cold, the elk, the pond.
Then something happens,
like electricity
through the beach that
turns the sand to glass
and shatters into
some strange courage
somewhere between myself
and who I want to be.

It's time, I think.
I need to tell her.

What Happens Next

Lisa, I think I love you.

She looks at me.

No, you don't, she says.

She holds both my hands,
stays quiet for a long time.

You think you do, she says.

....

You love me
because I love you.
You are like my brother.
My only real friend.
Because you're one of the only people
I've ever known who loves me for more than this.
She lets go and steps back,
waves her hand over her body.

> For a while, we stare at the ocean,
> watch the waves break into the sand.

She cries a little, softly.
You and your mom,
you love me no matter what,
like I'm a real person.
You let me be a kid.
The world sees me one way,
ever since I was little,
I had to be like a grown-up,
looking after my mom,
dealing with all of her boyfriends.

She pauses, crosses her arms,
looks toward the ocean
into some memory,
> then she starts again.

You guys see me for who I am.
I love you, Ari,
because even though
you didn't hear from me,

you expected me to be here,
like a friend should be.

I want to believe her,
but the words pour out anyway.
   Is it because I'm too big?

She shakes her head.
It never mattered to me
what you look like.
I care about you,
and I'm proud of you.
You're trying be healthy,
trying to be a better you.

She smiles at me,
like she's desperate
for me to understand.

You think you're mad at me for kissing that boy—
   Why did you? I interrupt.
It's not about you, Ari.
She raises her voice
like she's talking out
into the universe,
past me and everything else.
I'm so sorry, Ari.
I didn't think about how
it might hurt you.
That kiss was nothing.
I'm used to doing things on my own.
I have to make my own decisions.

I'm not used to having
someone looking out for me.

She looks me in the eyes.

I think about her mom.
I think about my father.
I think that maybe this
could be the end
of our friendship.

Please just forget about that, she says.
I look down.
She walks toward me slowly,
takes my hands.

I'm sorry, she whispers.
You're looking for something, Ari,
but I don't think it's me.
What do you mean? I ask.
She looks me in the eyes, and this time I see her.

It can't be me you're looking for, Ari,

because I'm your true friend,

and I

am already

here.

The Kiss

She's right.
Her words swirl in my gut.

In the movie of this,
I put my arm around her waist
and dip her backward
and kiss her into the sunset.
Instead I say, *You're right.*
She laughs. She points to the waves,
to the trees, to the town
sinking slowly into twilight.

We rest in a truth that
only we know,
friendship built
out of difficult circumstances,
chance, something more.
She puts her arms
around her body,
and she looks toward the water.

Lisa laughs and uncrosses her arms.
She walks toward me,
then she touches my hair.

But so we aren't curious forever . . .
She moves in closer,
holds my hands at first
then rests them low on her hips,
and her eyes overtake me.
I smell her breath and her soap,

her hair against my cheek.
Her lips are gravity,
and slowly they press to mine, so soft.

I don't know how long it lasts,
but when it stops, I know she can read my body,
feel it every single way.
She pulls me tighter until I feel so close,
the deep press of something changed forever.
Her hands slide into mine.
    Breathe.   Smile.
She turns, and we sit in the sand
and silently we watch
the sun go down.
We build a tiny wall
of sand between us,
just high enough
to be friends again.

                 Then

Did you know, I say,
*that there are four places
in England and New Jersey
where fish and frogs rained
down from the sky?*

No way! she says.
I draw maps in the sand
to make sure we don't miss
any detail.

That Part, Right Before Falling Asleep

So tired,
we rest in the twilight
of the planting room.
We try to talk
about everything we can.
I still feel
the crush
on my heart,
      but I know it's changing.

We lay our mats back to back
and stare up at all the drawings.

Tell me more, she says,
about the pond and the elk.

Tell me how you feel
      without the book.

Quiet

August has the warmest water,
the biggest waves.
We sit on the sand,
eating ham-and-cheese roll-ups.

I feel something
I haven't felt before.

Quiet.

It's quiet in my body.
No wishes
or name-calling
in my mind.

It's becoming what it's supposed to be.

As long as I can
remember, it was about
wishing for a different body.

All summer it seemed
to be about
making it disappear,
but I'm done hiding behind lies,
or too much skin,
or trying to be something else.

I pour the summer through my mind.
A breeze is blowing,
everything pond quiet,
redwood strong,
the wind through the trees,
        nothing else to lose.

The Revolution Inside

I walk by the pizza place,
smell the melting mozzarella,
the sauce, pepperoni,
and oregano.

For the first time, I don't
feel the need to rush in
or the fear that I won't get enough.

I don't *miss* the book,
or the rules or levels
or counting almonds
or forgetting the taste
of bread and chips.
The book was a guide,
but I'm not afraid to be without it,
and it feels free.
Like the revolution *is* inside me,
it's part of me now.
        A new appetite,
a new body, a new mind
that knows more
about how to do the right
things for myself.

Later that night,
we go for dinner,
celebrate our last days of summer.
We order a pizza
with olives and extra cheese.
I don't cut the crust off,
just happily eat
two of the slices,
                and it's enough.

The Game?

I miss Pick.
I'll have to email him
in Australia,
tell him the truth
about how I didn't do much with the game.
But I think he'll be happy
when I tell him about
all that's happened.
I think Pick
always believed in
me the most,
even if I do make
him mad sometimes.

I find our stack of folders
for the game near
Pick's abandoned
sleeping mat.

He is always
more organized
than I am,
makes sure that
things move forward.

I reach into
the top folder,
pull out a blank
sheet of graph paper,
and begin to sketch
something new:

us, on the beach,
tiny stick figures
on the sand,
and far from shore,
many graph-paper squares away,
a giant robot
stands in the ocean,
watching over us,
its massive frame
against the rising sun.

The Bruise Is Gone

At the beach,
Lisa's hand
moves along the intense
sunburn on my back.
That's stupid, she says.
Laughs. *You get this sunburn now?*

It's true. It's the first one of the summer.
She lets her hand glide down
at my side, rests it
on the shallowest part
of my love handle.

I can't see the bruise anymore, she says.
I feel a sudden tingle in my thumb,
the soreness from when
I pinched myself bloody.
The blue-black is all faded now,
the indentation gone,

my skin,
      all one color.

She lets her hand rest there
for a while, lets me feel it
until my body stops trembling.

New Beginning

Good news!
There's a gallery
on Hayes Street,
in the city.

My mother puts her phone down
and paints the scene with her hands.

They want to show my work.
The Lotus Keeper *and* Melinda,
some of the new paintings.
They even want me
to do some live exhibitions.

Lisa walks straight to *Melinda*
and whispers something into
her ear, makes a mean face.
Later, I turn the base of the sculpture
around so *Melinda*
can see the other side
of the gallery
for at least a little while
before she moves
to her new home.

One More Hike

One last morning,
we hike up the Dipsea Trail
toward Steep Ravine.
Not too far, just high enough
to see the ocean against the town,
the small buildings, and the long
stretch of sand against
the endless blue-green.

I don't hate school, Lisa says,
but I wish I only had
Shapiro's art classes.
I'm looking forward to those.

She asks me what I think.
I don't know. English is fun,
and sometimes science, and maybe
I can play sports or something?

We walk in silence
for a while, and I remember
that Lisa doesn't always go to school.
Do you think we'll hang out?
I think in terms of worst-case scenario,
just in case.

Probably not, she says.

Silence.

....

We laugh.
She hits my arm, then hugs me quickly.
I'll be around.

    More silence.

How do you think you'll feel that first day?
I don't know, I say.
I kind of want people to be like, NO WAY!
We laugh more, look out at the Pacific.
What about, you know?
She means Frank and the boys from the bike path.
I don't say anything. I don't mention their names.
You know, Ari, she says, *you really have changed.*
Her eyes are so clear.

She looks out across
the water,
her mind far away,
to whatever happens next.

She laughs.
Didn't the book say
to take an after picture?
Maybe you should,
even if it's just to remember
this summer.

After Picture

We stand on the deck again,
in the same way we did
at the start of the summer.

Jorge walks in
and puts his
long arms around me and Lisa
while my mom takes the picture.

Lisa prints
it right away, smiles at me,
but I don't look at it.

A Last Look

I look at the mirror
in the nursery bathroom
one last time.

There's less of me,
but I'm not
an action hero.
I can still feel the slight
overhang of my belly on my shorts,
the dig of the elastic,
and the skin on the backs of my arms,
especially soft. I've gained
back a few pounds, but it's okay.

So much less of me.
So much more of me too.

What would the diet doctor say?
Or my father,

who hasn't really seen me
go through this change at all?

It doesn't matter,
because I like myself.
All of myself.
Cryptozoologist,
mountain survivor,
boogie boarder,
someone with friends
who care about me.

I dig my feet into the warm sand,
Lisa next to me, laughing,
the spray of the ocean,
sudden and alive.

I look back toward the mountains.
I've been in there,
and I feel the ache
of my wet feet along the trails,
and out toward the sea,
in the horizon,
is the promise
of becoming
something more
than who I am now
or something else
that I don't have to ever be again.

Dropping Lisa Off

When we reach Miller Avenue,
she takes my hand,
lifts it up to her forehead.
I don't waaannnnt to say good-bye,
she cries, in her exaggerated, whiny voice.

We turn onto Throckmorton.
Lisa's mom is standing outside,
smiling. She runs to the car,
opens the door.
We all get out
in a sea of hugs.
Lisa shows
her the paintings from the summer.

After a while, the Artist
takes Lisa by the arm,
and they walk away for a few moments
beneath the old redwoods.

There's crying
and a few words not for any other ears,
and as they walk back,
Lisa's head rests on the Artist's shoulder.
Then Lisa hugs her tightly,
and the moms go off together
for a little while.

Inside Lisa's room,
I stare at all the pictures
of Def Leppard,

Foo Fighters, dragons
and Pegasus, and warriors
we've drawn together.
I have a million questions
I want to ask her
about the future.

We make plans.

We'll meet
before school
near the clock tower
by the flower beds.

She looks at me,
You know you will always be my friend,
even when I don't make it to school.
Don't forget. She leans in,
kisses me on the forehead.

I feel the perfect weight
of her hand on my neck.

I know,
          I say.
Promise? she asks.
I really do.

On the way out, I hear her laughing as she yells out,
You should call Gretchen.

After Summer

— ## Gretchen

We meet at
the vintage record store
in Larkspur.
I know it's her
in a pea-green
military jacket,
striped leggings,
and brown boots.

It took me one hour
to decide what to wear,
my confidence a little
shaken by gaining back
a few pounds.
I try to find a perfect
combination

but end up with
jeans and a white
Hawaiian shirt
with green flowers.

Her hair is orange,
Pippi Longstocking
pigtails
beneath her fuzzy
black fedora.

She is so tall,
taller than me.

When I walk up to her,
she looks slowly over
and smiles.

Then, without even stopping,
she puts her long arms out
and hugs me right away.

Like, finally!
she says.
She holds up
Purple Rain.
You already have this, right?
But have you heard this?
She holds up "Blue Jean,"
an old David Bowie single.

We walk aisle to aisle,
looking through records,

holding the album covers up,
talking about every design,
how crazy and awesome
people look
or how much makeup
the singer wears.

Her freckles
really do fill up
her whole face.
I'm a full cup
of orange juice,
she tells me later.

We walk outside
and look at the other shops
and talk, and it's just like
it was on the phone.
Better.

By the fountain,
after we drop in five pennies each
and talk about whether these
wishes really work,
she puts both hands on my shoulders.
So what do you think of me?
She's not pushy, just funny,
nice, her smile contagious
with her huge teeth,
and warm eyes.
Good? I say.
Good? Whatever.
She laughs.

....

You're totally cute, Ari.

The words spin
around my body.
I can't remember anyone
ever saying this to me.

We walk randomly
until we see
her dad's minivan.
He waves, and she smiles,
squeezes my hand,
and walks toward the car.
I watch her go,
and I can't stop smiling,
But then halfway, she turns,
runs back.
She hugs me and whispers
                    in my ear,

                              Told you you'd like me.

She gets in the van,
waves through the window
as it drives away.
I wait in the warm afternoon
for my mother.

                              She's right.

Later, inside the record jacket
I find a red piece

of paper with three little words
in black writing.
When I read them,
I hear her silly, happy voice saying,

Call me soon.

Tallit

I walk straight to the desk,
turn the snow globe over,
pull two saltwater taffies
from the bowl.

I'm sorry, Rabbi,
I didn't get to practice much.

The rabbi shrugs,
disappointed, and stares at me.
He rubs his hand on his beard.
Ari, it's not going to learn itself.

I make promises to study,
I say the prayers more boldly,
I tell the rabbi about the pond,
about dropping the book
into the water.
I tell him that I think
I am changing.

He listens closely to every word,
quietly nodding,
looking at me through
his glasses.

Twice a week, Ari?
Okay?

He asks me if I'm ready for school.
I think so, I say,
but I'm not sure.
In this moment,
I want to tell him
what happened
on the bike path,
but I don't.
I want to ask
him if he thinks
that I have to fight
to be a man,
but I think I already
know the answer.

The rabbi walks to the wardrobe
in the corner of his study.
He hums a song under his breath,
his voice rising and falling
with every movement of his body.

He pulls a folded white
cloth from the top shelf,
brings it over to the chairs,
and unfolds it.

Piece by piece, he drapes
the wool garment, blue- and white-
and black-striped, over my shoulders.

This tallit is for you, Ari,
for when the time comes.

I feel the warmth of the cloth,
the perfect heaviness of the material,
like being watched over.

The rabbi makes sure
I have all the recordings
I need so I can practice.
He folds the tallit,
puts it back on the shelf.
He shakes my hand,
smiles. I will be back.

I ride my bike
as fast as I can
down the steep
San Francisco hills,
the fog and cool air
in my face,
prayers humming
on my lips.

First Day of School

We drive over the bridge.
I feel the magnetic pull of Shoreline Highway
as we pass the turnoff to Stinson,
but instead we go straight, toward school.

Yesterday, we went shopping.
I bought three pairs
of pants and one pair of ripped jeans.

34/32.

I wear the jeans
and a long-sleeved black T-shirt,
tan Converse All Stars,
and a new gray backpack.

On my right,
the bike path stretches
across the morning.
Herons fly
across the estuary.
Soon enough, I think,
I will be back on my bike.
I'm not sure if I'm any tougher
or if I'd do it any differently now.
I don't know if I will tell
anyone else what happened,
or even if I should.

I think about how much
I wish Pick was here
too, but he's still in Australia
until Christmas. We email a lot,
work on the game. But it's not the same.

Mom puts her hand on mine.
Are you sure you want to take the bus home today?

Yes. I smile.

I'm so proud of you, Ari.
She hugs me, and I step
foot by foot out the door and
into a sea of drop-off cars.

It's foggy but bright,
and everything is twice the speed.

I see Noah first thing.
His long, purple-striped rugby shirt
same as always.
Hey, Noah, I say.
He stops. Looks at me.
Whoa, he says, *dude, you're so tall!*

Look at you.

Diana walks around the corner.
Ari! Youlooksogoodohmygodddddd.
Her smile makes me smile.

I can see others looking at me,
and I take it all in.

Then,
    all of a sudden,

I see Frank walking up
from the parking lot.
I feel my shirt, loose

on my body, but I
still suck it in.

Habit.

He gets closer,
and I feel
my body tighten
in memory,
adrenaline like a fist.
    Maybe I *could* stand up to him.
    I get ready,
    fists at my side,

        but then he
        just walks by me,

and that's when I see it.
His eyes shift,
looking down and away,
the collar of his polo shirt turned up
trying to cover what looks like
a bad sunburn over his whole face—

                acne everywhere.

He stops and looks at me,
looks around at the campus.
He smiles a little,
but he mostly looks terrified.
Hey, um, Ari? He coughs. *I'm sorry about
what happened.* He doesn't
look me in the eye.

            . . . .

I think of all the things I want to say,
should say,
    but instead
                I just say,
                        Okay.
That's it. Frank lingers for a few seconds
like he might say something else,
but instead he just walks away.

Wow, Noah says,
talk about looking different.
I shake my head.
I can't believe it.

But most of all,
it surprises me how many
people *don't* notice,
because in my mind,
I had made this day about me,
when really it's about all of us.
A new time, a new place,
new . . . us.

Friends No Matter What

Noah heads to woodshop,
his early elective,
and I remember the plan
to meet Lisa.

I walk up the stairs toward the base
of the clock tower near the flower beds.

Slowly the other students slip
away toward the first classes of the day.

I don't see her,
and I remember
that she's unpredictable
and it's not her fault.
She doesn't owe me anything.
I hear her voice,
reminding me

    we are friends no matter what.

I wait there
near the flower beds,
the sun and the fog
pouring into the morning,
until the clock tower
sounds the second bell,
and when she doesn't come,
I head to English.

The Phone Call

I run home from the bus stop.
I've had so many new ideas for the game.
I need to get back to it.
Plus, Gretchen said she
would call me on Thursday.

It's Thursday.

The city is cold,
fall setting in all the way.
I zip up my jacket,
run from Chestnut Street
down toward Divisadero,
up the stairs
and inside.

I throw my backpack
on the counter.
There's a note there
from Mom, telling me
she'll be home from
the gallery before dinner.
    She tries so hard to be a good mom.

I open a diet soda,
eat a piece of Muenster cheese,
tearing off the yellow edges
piece by piece,
and a few saltines.

On the counter is a troll
I made in the summer.
He's holding a boogie board
on top of his head,
crooked legs and crooked teeth.
I think about summer all the time.

Suddenly the phone rings,
and I swallow the cheese,
take a sip of soda.
        Gretchen!

I clear my throat,
and try to think of the right words
to start things off.

Near the phone
are the two photos.
The *before* picture,
where we smile in the sun.

    I see Pick and Lisa,
    bright in the sunshine,
    and I think of Jorge too,

    so real and unreal at the same time.
Next to it, the *after* picture, turned facedown.
I smile at them.
                 Both are me.
                              All the way.
I pick up the phone,

      take a breath,

but it's so quiet.

Hello? I say.

    Silence.

Hello? And then something unexpected,
a voice, scratchy and familiar,
hurried. A voice like Central Park
or learning to ride my bike.
A voice
    like home.

....

Ari? it finally whispers. I stop breathing, and again,
               Ari?
                           I let the breath in, slowly, and find
my voice.

         Dad?

It's a start.

Home

My mom declares,
It's time to clean,
spends the afternoon
putting every spray bottle,
brush, sponge,
and mop out on the kitchen
counter and starts to work.
This is her magic way
of making things new.

In the hallway,
I wipe the baseboards,
and down in the cracks
I see the pounds I've lost,
like creatures
hiding there,
waiting to
reach out
with sugary tentacles
and bready arms,

trying to get back on
my chin,
my love handles,
my belly,
my brain.
I spray them with
all-purpose cleaner,
dissolve them back
into the crevices.

I go to the scale,
weigh myself,
and some of the pounds did hang on,
                                    7 of them.
I think about this for a long time.
At first, I feel the desperate rush
to find a new copy of *The Diet Book*.
Then I feel the compulsion to eat something
        sweet.

I walk into my room,
already cleaned,
my desk spread full of drawings,
markers, and graph paper.
My shelves full of books,
a small clay troll holding ten-sided dice
and a framed drawing
of Elysium leaning on her silver sword.

I think, a few weeks ago,
        gaining some weight back
                would have felt like failure,
                like I might as well just give up.

But it's different now.

I don't give up.

I don't.
Because it isn't just
about filling up on food.
Inside my skin
is the beach, and the sand,
the redwoods and pond water,
the feel of a kiss, wet on my lips,
a mountain climbed,
and fog forever,
boogie boards,
and sleeping mats,
stories and stories,
and real

friends.

None of it
heavy water.
Just me moving forward,
finding my own story.

I look in the mirror
near my desk,
pull up my shirt.
I see the slight bump
of my love handles,
the extra space
of my slight double chin,
but I also see how I look
different, and it's not just
about the weight anymore.

....

I am
more myself than ever.

I can't control everything—
my father, or Lisa, or anyone else—

but I can be healthier,
I can take care of myself,
I can *be* myself.

I'm okay.
I am

me.

Acknowledgments

Thank you to all the "real-life" people who play a part in this work of fiction, standing up and standing with me through some of the most difficult times in my life.

I am grateful beyond measure for my incredible agent, Rena Rossner, for loving this manuscript even in its earliest drafts and for working so hard to get it right. Thank you, most of all, for believing in me. Thanks to editor extraordinaire, Liz Szabla, for working tirelessly with me, for poring over the verse, for taking such incredible care of Ari and his friends, and for honoring me as a writer all the way through the process. It is a privilege to work with you. Thanks to the whole team at Feiwel & Friends, Anna Poon, publicist Kelsey Marrujo, and creative director Rich Deas. Thanks to production editor Lindsay Wagner and production manager Kim Waymer. Thanks to the amazing cover artist Chris Sheban for capturing the spirit of the book! Of course, thank you to Jean Feiwel for your warmth and your vision, for making me feel so at home at F&F. Thanks to Matt de la Peña for shaking up my life in the best way, for all the years of support, guidance, and friendship.

Thank you to the teachers, librarians, and educators out there who put books in the hands of kids who need them and for standing up for *all* children every day and teaching them they have a place in this world no matter what.

Thanks to those educators in the San Diego State University MFA program and beyond who believed in me as a writer and taught me that my words matter—Sandra Alcosser, Marilyn Chin, Glover Davis, and so many others. Thank you to my colleagues and students at San Diego City College and, of course, the English Center, who I have the privilege of working with side by side every day. You inspire me endlessly.

An immense thank you to my unbelievable community of deep friends and family who believe in me all the way.

Thank you to my writing people, writers whose love knows no bounds at all—Heather Eudy, Cali Linfor, Sabrina Youmans, and Nancy Cary—for reading every version of this manuscript, and for so many days and nights of hard questions, laughing, and crying. Thank you to my editor/writer friends—Crystal Ellefsen, Alan Traylor, and Adam Heine— for your enthusiasm and love for this book. Thank you also to the incredible community of writers I have grown with over this past year—Rena's Renegades, my debut group; the Novel-Nineteens; the #JPStreetteam; #KIDSNEEDMENTORS; and the unbelievable world of Middle Grade and YA authors who care so much for kids and for one another. You bring me so much hope. Thank you for your friendship.

Thank you to all the wise sages in my life—Bob; Maggie; Emmett; Randall; my brother, Steve; Tuesday Morning crew; and so many others—who keep me on the right path.

I am grateful for all the friendships and landscapes from my own childhood years that are woven into my heart and the heart of this book: New York City and PS 6, San Francisco, Mill Valley and Mill Valley Middle School, and Stinson Beach.

Thank you to my own mother, the artist, who, despite all of life's challenges, championed art, creativity, feminism, freedom of expression, and taught me that nothing is impossible and that *all* people are worth it. So much of this book is for you.

Thank you to my son, Asa, and my daughters, Samaria and Caylao, for healing me, and filling my life with joy I can't measure. You are my favorite human beings. Thank you for being so understanding during all the times that I had to "go and write."

And most of all, thank you to my beautiful and fearless wife, Ella, for her unconditional love and support for me, for this book, and for this life we have built together. I am grateful every day.

Lastly, thank you to all the kids out there, just like Ari, whose stories have inspired me to write this book. I believe with all my heart that you can change the world!